The Taker
The Adventures of Silver Dove, Book Ten
Eliza Scalia

Copyright © **2023 Eliza Scalia**

Published by: Winged Publications

Cover Illustration by: Katherine Lauren
Based upon the characters originally designed by Suji Gallianetti and the further work by Wayne F. Shurtz and Cheyanne and Jean Buffkin

This book is a work of fiction. Names, characters, places, and incidents are the product of the author's imagination and are used fictitiously. Any resemblance to actual events, locales, or persons, living or dead, is coincidental.

No part of this book may be copied or distributed without the author's consent.

All rights reserved.
ISBN: 978-1-959788-75-1

Dedicated to so many that I grew up with, who faced the problem that Andre has within this story.

Chapter One
Colomba-
A Cold Day

The cold wind seems to cut straight through my sweater, sending goosebumps all over my body. I shiver as I try to blow warm air onto my hands. This only gives me a little warmth that quickly fades away as the wind continues to pick up. I am walking on the sidewalk downtown, heading to the diner so that I can hang out with my friends Nat and Luis. Even though I am bundled up, I still feel like a walking popsicle. From the smell in the air, I can guess that we may be getting snow pretty soon, something I would love. I have always enjoyed the snow, no matter how cold it gets, I still have to play in the snow. Making snow forts, snow angels, and having snow ball fights are some of the most fun things you can do during the winter.

As these happy thoughts go through my mind, I turn around a corner and my happy thoughts leave my head as I hear a roar of a car engine behind me, I glance back to see a shiny red sports car slowly approaching me. I have to hide a groan because I know who is the one driving that stupid fancy car. Alex pulls up to the curb right beside me, with two of his football team buddies in the car with him. They all look comfortable in the heated car while I shiver on the sidewalk.

"Hey gorgeous, need a ride?" Alex asks with his usual confident grin. He has been trying to give me a ride ever since he got this new car for his birthday a few weeks ago. With his family being rich, it's not surprising that they gave him such a nice car, I just wish that he would stop trying to show off with it. Even though I am tempted to get in the car to get warm, I give him my refusal.

"No thanks, I'm almost where I need to go anyway." Alex just chuckles at that.

"Aw c'mon Colomba, we can take you somewhere you can have a lot more fun. Come on!" Even though he's trying to sound cool in front of his friends, I can hear the desperation hidden behind his tone. He really wants me to go with him, and I can't help but pity him a little bit, but there's no way that I will back out on plans I've made with my friends.

"No Alex, I'm fine." I try to sound stern with my answer so that he can take a hint, but apparently this guy's hint detector is broken in that tiny brain of his.

"C'mon Colomba, a pretty little thing like you shouldn't be walking around in the cold, I can keep you warm in here." I almost puke at what he says, but instead I start walking again as I call out to him.

"No thanks Alex, I'm good!" I cross the street and enter the diner, instantly grateful for the heating inside. As soon as I entered the diner, I could hear the roar of the engine again as Alex sped off down the street, as if he was trying to make me regret my decision of not going with him. As if I would ever regret that. I roll my eyes before putting a smile on my face as I walk over to the table that my friends are already sitting at. Nat is currently munching on some French fries as she talks to our other friend Luis. Luis chuckles as she tells him a joke. Nat notices me and waves me over, Luis immediately stops laughing to look back at me, smiling warmly as he waves at me too. I wave back as I walk over to the table and sit down beside Luis.

"Hey guys, did I miss anything interesting?" Nat shakes her head at me.

"Nah, not really." She looks me over for a minute, a look of concern passing over her face. "What's up with you? Why do you look so annoyed?" I groan a little at the thought of what just happened only moments ago.

"Oh, I just had another run in with Alex." Luis straightens up a bit more as anger flashes through his gaze.

"What did he do now?" I hear a faint growl in his voice that sounds threatening, almost as if he wants to hurt someone. The tone he spoke in makes my heart race a bit even though I know that I have nothing to fear when it comes to Luis, but sometimes when that tone gets into his voice, it can be frightening. I clear my throat awkwardly to get rid of that negative feeling, he's my best friend, I shouldn't think about stuff like that.

"Nothing much, still just trying to flirt and show off." The darkness in his brown eyes lightens up as he chuckles softly.

"I'm guessing that roar we heard was his new car, wasn't it?" This time it is my turn to chuckle.

"Yep, he was trying to offer me a ride, even when I told him no, he kept trying to convince me saying that he could show me a better time than whatever it was that I had planned." The darkness instantly returns to Luis' gaze, and he takes a drink of his coffee, probably to give him a moment to calm down before he speaks again. I can see that he has a lot of anger built up in him at the remark I made, his hand is holding onto his coffee cup so tightly that I'm afraid he will shatter the cup. When he is done taking a sip, he looks over at me and tries to smile through his anger.

"That guy really can't just take a hint, can he? A guy really needs to know how to respect it when a girl says no. Says a lot about him as a man if he can't do that." Nat nods her head at what Luis said.

"It really does. It feels like Alex has been chasing after you forever Colomba, you would think that he would take a hint by now. I mean, he started chasing you ever since we started high school, didn't he?" I nod my head while Luis laughs darkly.

"A guy like him never gets a hint if it means he doesn't get what he wants. The guy is pretty ruthless. If he wants something, he will make sure he gets it." What he says sends a shiver of terror through me since I know that what he means is that Alex is willing to do anything to have me. Luis must have felt my shiver since his face softens instantly, seeing that I am a bit upset. Resting his hand on top of mine, he smiles comfortingly at me. "Don't worry Colomba, I won't let that creep do anything to you. I would rather die than let anything bad happen to you." I smile back at him, instantly forgetting my fear as I hug him to show my gratitude.

"Thanks Luis, you make me feel so safe." I whisper in his ear as we hold each other. I can feel his body relaxing in my embrace, and I start to relax as well. When we separate, I glance across the table at Nat to see her grinning at the two of us, like she knows a little secret. I look away from her, trying not to get annoyed again. I know why she was looking at us like that, she thinks that Luis likes me as more than a friend and that we would be a cute couple. Luis is just my friend though, so I won't even bother thinking about that kind of stuff. And I'm not going to talk about what Nat is obviously thinking, instead I decide to change the subject.

"So did you guys here about what happened to that one guy Paul Dalton in our math class?" They both tell me that they haven't, so I tell them all the strange story about how Paul nearly lost a hand in the wood shop in school just the other day. The three of us chat and have a great time together as the wind whistles outside, promising us an even colder day tomorrow.

Chapter Two
Luis-
Dark Thoughts
After The Diner

The wind tussles up my already messy hair, sending more of it into my face, covering my eyes. Glancing at myself in the reflection of a store window, I see a kid who is still hiding his face from the world with his hair even though he is the most powerful person in this town. Nobody would ever guess that though, they just see a pitiful little weakling. How is it that I have done so much destruction in this town, yet I am still such a pathetic thing?

Colomba, Nat, and I all just finished eating and are all heading home. Since the diner is downtown, I am just walking home to my uncle's apartment above his antique shop. It's only two blocks away, but in this cold weather it feels like miles. The cold wind blows through a few holes in my thin coat, making me shiver even more. Sticking a finger through one of the holes in my sleeve, a sudden wave of anger flows through me. My uncle and I may have enough money to survive, but that's pretty much it. We can't really afford to get new clothes, or even good clothes for that matter. I've had this coat the last three winters and I have grown a lot in that time. The sleeves don't even go down to my wrists, I have to wear extra-long gloves to make sure my arms don't get cold. Even when we were at the diner, I didn't tell Colomba or Nat this, but I made sure to get the cheapest thing on the menu. I couldn't spend much, but I also wanted to spend time with some friends like any normal teenager. The problem is that it's sometimes hard to have fun with friends if you don't have money to do the fun things. When you are broke you have to be creative to figure out how to have fun. When you have money it's easy, you can do whatever you please without having to worry about how much you spent.

A sudden roar like the growl of a massive monster comes from behind me, distracting me from my thoughts. Before I am able to get further from the street, the growling thing comes up from behind me and then crashes through a huge puddle beside me, spraying me with ice cold water mixed with snowy sludge. Through the tangled mess of my now wet hair, I see Alex high fiving one of his friends in his new car. It's obvious what just happened. Alex saw me and decided to cause me a little misery, so he drove his car right in a puddle just to spray me. I shake my head like a dog just getting out of a bath to try and get some water out of my hair, but it doesn't help that much.

The beautiful red sports car continues down the street, the three guys in the car laugh, probably about their little joke on me. They are all warm in that car while I am soaked and shivering. My hatred burns so coldly in me that I almost place my hand on the Crow Medal so that I can become the Crow and send my demon shadow dogs after them. My hand was only an inch away from touching it before the image of Colomba came into my head. She would be so disappointed in me if I gave into my anger like that and hurt someone. She has always told me that I am better than what I think of myself, I don't want her to start thinking that I am as terrible as I think I am. I lower my hand from the medal, watching with misery and jealousy as Alex and his friends drive away, probably going out to do something fun while I have to spend a boring evening at home.

  As I continue to make my way to the apartment, my now soaked shoes seem to squish on the sidewalk. My heart feels heavy as a single thought runs through my mind; there is so much that I would sacrifice to switch places with Alex, to be in a rich family that can afford to give me a nice car like that. To be able to go places with Colomba, to drive around with her to go on little adventures and get closer. I want to be able to live my life without worrying about whether or not my uncle and I will be able to afford to pay the rent on our apartment. I don't really have a regular job, but I do little odd jobs with the shops around my uncle's to get a few bucks here and there. It's not much but it helps my uncle pay the bills and that's what matters. I just wish we had more money so that I can do more with my life instead of working to get more money and worrying that I don't have enough.

When I make it into the shop, my uncle is talking to a customer about some old furniture so I just go upstairs to be by myself. As soon as I get there, I place my hand on the Crow Medal and Shadow instantly appears on my bedside table.

"Good afternoon Master, how are you feeling?" I smile when I hear her calm voice, she always has some kind of magical way to make my troubles seem to disappear. I go into my closet so that I can have the privacy I need to take off my soggy clothes. She may be a bird, but Shadow is still a girl.

"I feel okay considering what just happened with Alex." I tell her as I slip into my pajamas.

"Yes I saw what happened through your eyes." She states with some sadness now in her calm voice. "I'm sorry you had to experience that, but I also sensed some dark thoughts in your mind after it happened, and also when Colomba mentioned Alex trying to show off to her about his new car. Tell me, what was going through your head." I try to hide a sigh as I get out of the closet because I know that I will have to tell her the truth since I cannot hide from her.

"Honestly, I was thinking about how he has always had things handed to him while I've had to struggle to get anything. I can never really afford to get the stuff I want, while he can get it so easily. I just wish that I had money like him, that way I could have a nice car that I could offer to let Colomba ride around in. I know we could have so much fun if we didn't have to rely on our families to get us places." I scoff at myself, as I tell her the part that really bothers me. "With how things are right now, there's no way I could ever ask out a girl like Colomba. We could never really do anything together if I have no money to do anything with her. I can't take her anywhere, or get anything. And besides, who would want me as I am. I mean, who loves poor, pathetic kids like me? They hate me and want to let me suffer, at least that's how it seems based on the things that have happened to me in my life." Shadow softly sighs as she shakes her head in exasperation.

"You just never learn, do you? Just because you hate yourself doesn't mean that everyone else does too." I shrink back a little at her brutal honesty.

"Well despite what you say, people seem to have something against me for being who I am, considering I've been pushed down my whole life. I mean it could be because they think I'm weak, or I'm weird, or because I'm poor. I don't know, it could be a mix of all three, either way, the world seems to hate me as I am." I turn away from her and look out the window, trying to show her that I want to end this conversation. Outside I see people in their cars, driving around and enjoying their day. Some wander into some of the shops downtown to buy things that I could never afford and to eat at the restaurants that I can never get into. I watch them, feeling jealous as I see them enjoy the things I will never get to have.

Chapter Three
Colomba-
Home Again

The soapy water from the dishes I'm washing covers my hands while I scrub a very dirty pot that Nonna used to make a Korean dish that I have no idea how to pronounce. It is completely silent in the kitchen around me. We all finished dinner a little bit ago, so my dad is in his study reading a book while Nonna is in the living room working on a new quilt. Since it is so quiet, my mind races through everything that happened today.

I had such a great time with Luis and Nat at the diner, but it feels like it was almost ruined all thanks to Alex. It's almost impressive that Alex could almost ruin our day since he wasn't even around everyone, but Alex does seem to have a talent for ruining things. Just mentioning Alex put Luis in a bad mood. I know that Alex and Luis hate each other, but neither of them have ever explained to me why they are like that. Apparently, they have gone to school with each other ever since they were little, so there is a lot that could have happened between them since then. Based on things that have been said, Alex bullies Luis a lot, which is one of the many reasons why I will never be friends with Alex.

I know that this is rude of me to think about my friend, but I think another thing that makes them not like each other is the fact that Luis seems to be a bit jealous of Alex. It's pretty easy to see why; Alex is good looking, is popular with practically everyone (especially the girls), he's athletic, and everything always seems to go his way. The thing about Alex that seemed to bother Luis the most today though is that Alex's family has money while Luis and his uncle always seem to be struggling to survive. Luis' parents and uncle came to this country with practically nothing, and they have been fighting hard to make it ever since. Luis always comes to school with old clothes, while Alex comes in wearing only the best, which makes all the girls fawn all over him. Luis seemed upset today that Alex was trying to show off his new car to me again. I stop working on the dishes for a moment as a sudden thought hits me. Was Luis mad that Alex was showing off the car, or was he mad that Alex was showing it off to me?

I shake my head, I'm thinking too highly of myself right now. Luis is my best friend, just because he's a boy doesn't mean that he likes me like that. What on earth was I thinking? I've known Luis for a few years now, if he had those kinds of feelings for me, he would have told me, or I would have noticed. There's no way that he feels that way towards me. He would be a wonderful boyfriend for someone, but I suppose that will never be me. A sudden feeling of sadness comes over me at that thought. It almost is like the feeling I had when the Flying Ace got rid of her spell on me that made me fall in love with Luis. Back then, I felt bad because we were no longer in love, now I feel sad because I know that he doesn't love me.

I shake my head, trying to get rid of that thought. I scrub the pot harder, trying to get rid of some of the frustration I feel. Luis is my best friend, I can't have thoughts like this, we are friends and that's it, nothing more and nothing less.

As I think about Luis, the reason I started thinking of him in the first place comes back to my mind, his jealousy with Alex. Alex gets to show off his fancy car to the world, while Luis doesn't have anything really to show off, except his talent for art of course. Luis doesn't talk about it much, but I know he and his uncle are poor. I wish I could help, but I know that they are too proud to let me help them. Even though they don't have much, they never let that make them cold, they have always been warm people. One thing I can say about Alex, is that I think being rich has made him a worse person. That guy thinks that he can buy anything... or anyone for the right price. He obviously thought that he could buy my attention just by driving around in that fancy car. If he thinks I can be bought so easily, he's got another thing coming. If Luis suddenly got a lot of money though, I don't think if would ruin him, he would probably be the same wonderful human being he already is. I don't think anything could corrupt him.

That thought sends a warm feeling all through

me that is instantly cut short when one memory enters my mind. I think back to when all three of us were at the diner and Luis got mad when I told them about Alex trying to show off. He had such a dark look on his face, a face full of hatred and fury. Now that I think of it, I've seen that expression on his face multiple times, almost every single time I think we were talking about Alex. I always thought they hated each other, but after thinking about how Luis looks when we talk about Alex, now it seems like it is something more than hatred. Some times when he gets that look in his eyes, I seriously think that Luis has the potential to really hurt someone, something I never thought Luis would be capable of.

I turn on some music to try and get rid of these scary thoughts, but no matter what I do, I can't get the menacing look in his eyes out of my brain. No matter what I do for the rest of the evening, those dark eyes haunt me, even when I try to go to sleep. As my eyes close, I know that those eyes will haunt my nightmares.

Chapter Four
Luis-
The Group

Even though I am inside the school, I am still bundled up. It almost feels as if the cold outside has stuck to my bones. Guess that's what I get for being poor and not being able to buy a coat good enough for this kind of weather. Right now, outside it is doing that weird thing that's between snow and rain. So not only does it not have the prettiness of snow, but it is also damp and makes you wet and freezing, the perfect combo for getting a cold, which is what I'm expecting by the end of the day.

The school day has ended, but I am still stuck here for a little bit since my uncle has a few appointments and said he will pick me up later. For now, I'm just wandering the halls, trying to kill some time. Colomba is still at school too, but she can't hang out with me right now since she is helping out with the tutoring. She is teaching Alex again since his father apparently pays extra so that he can have her specifically. I know Colomba hates teaching him since he tries to flirt with her the whole time, but she gets paid well so she tries her best to ignore his flirting and teach him as best as she can. That is one of the many things I admire about her, she doesn't give up no matter what annoying things she has to deal with. I will admit though, that I am annoyed that she has to deal with him.

Alex doesn't even treat Colomba like he thinks of her as a human being, he just looks at her as a pretty girl he wants to date. He just looks at her beautiful aquamarine eyes, he doesn't see the kind soul behind those eyes. He sees her angel like face, but he doesn't see the gentleness she has in each expression. He sees nothing but a pretty face that he wants to have for his own and show off with, not someone who truly wants to spend his time with. Ever since the start of high school, he has been chasing her and trying to keep her away from me. He knows that I like her, and he wants her all for himself. Even though Colomba and I are just friends, he can't accept that. He made that perfectly clear every day we were in art class together our freshman year, and every day since then.

Wait… art class? A wave of annoyance suddenly hits me as I realize a stupid mistake I made earlier today. I keep a small bag of pencils in my backpack, I forgot it in my advanced art class earlier today. I'm sure that if Mr. Sizemore saw that I left it behind he held onto it for me, he's a cool guy like that. I have had him teaching me in different art classes since I started at this school, he is my all time favorite teacher. I head straight to his classroom, knowing that he won't mind me coming in and chatting for a second while I grab my pencil bag.

After all my time here, I don't even have to think about where his classroom is, I could get there with my eyes closed if I wanted to. I make it there in no time flat, and knock on the door before immediately walking in.

"Hey Mr. Sizemore, sorry to butt in like this, but I forgot my-" As soon as I actually look in the classroom, my blood freezes in my veins when I see that there are quite a few other people there, practically all of them are people I know. I know them, but not in a friendly kind of way. In front of me, sitting with their chairs in a circle, facing each other with a lady in the center that I do not know, are all of the people I have transformed as the Crow. All of them are there, except Alex.

They are all staring at me as if they are expecting something. Wait, do they know who I really am? Is that why they are all looking at me like this? Are they here to confront me, or are they here to thank me for everything I have done for them? As I look around at all of their faces, they don't look upset or happy that I am here, just like they are waiting for something. It feels like a century passes before I realize the obvious, they don't know who I really am, they are just looking at me because I entered the room and interrupted whatever it is they are doing.

"Uh… hi. I'm sorry I barged in like this, I was just looking for Mr. Sizemore."

"Oh hey Luis, I'm in here." I look over to the back of the classroom to see Mr. Sizemore coming out of the art room's supply closet. "Sorry about that, I was just organizing some of the supplies. What do you need?" He smiles at me in his usual friendly manner, which helps me feel a bit better about the awkward situation I created with barging in.

"I left my pencil bag in here earlier today, have you seen it?" Mr. Sizemore nods his head.

"Oh yeah, I grabbed it for you when I saw that you left it behind. It's on my desk." He points over to his desk and I see it next to his coffee cup. I start walking over to pick it up when Mr. Sizemore keeps talking. "We were just getting started with this session if you wish to join in, I feel like you might be able to add on to the conversation." I pick up the pencil bag, feeling a wave of confusion come over me.

"A session for what?" I glance back at the woman in the room that the people I have transformed are all circled around. She smiles at me when she sees my confusion, and gives me a calm, yet confusing answer.

"This is a therapy session for those who have been affected by the Crow and what he has done in this school. You can join if you like." My stomach feels like it has been suddenly been filled with rocks, I want to puke, but my body feels too heavy to be able to get it out. I know that I should just get out of this room as fast as possible, but something holds my feet to the ground. I'm curious. I want to know what they will say about me, I want to see how I have helped the people I have transformed.

"Okay." I pull up a chair and put myself into the circle. Even though everyone greets me with pleasant smiles, a dark feeling comes over me and I can't help but wonder if I made the right decision.

When I sit down, I look at the lady who, I guess, is the therapist leading this session. When I look at her, she somehow seems familiar. Have I seen her around town sometime? The woman is pretty young, probably in her early or mid-twenties. She has very dark hair that is cut really short, Colomba once told me that the style is called a pixie cut. She has a black scarf with very intricate patterns in her hair to keep it away from her face. She is dressed in black as well, she has a flowing black skirt and a black hooded sweater, definitely not the "professional" look I would expect from a therapist. What makes her look even less professional is that around her neck is what looks like a dog fang hanging from a necklace. When I look into her eyes though, I am instantly mesmerized by them. Her eyes are so dark that they could be completely black, I can't even tell the difference between the colored part of her eyes with her pupil. She looks straight into my eyes with the dark, void like emptiness of her gaze. I feel like she is trying to absorb everything within my mind with her eyes; taking all of my ideas, memories, and feelings. I am so entranced by her eyes that it takes me a moment to realize that she is asking me a question.

"I'm sorry, but what did you say?"

"Miss Corbeau was asking you if you feel comfortable enough to tell everyone about your own personal story about your experience with the Crow." Kal says beside me. I quickly look over him to see that he has changed a bit since I transformed him into the Giant. He was getting bullied because he was overweight, now I can see that he has lost quite a bit of weight. He isn't thin yet, but he is obviously working on it and is making progress.

"Well, I don't really have too much to say, I guess. I have had the same experience as most people; Crow comes around, I run and hide somewhere until it is over." I keep my eyes down, feeling a bit embarrassed lying right to the faces of these people. I feel so weak having to lie even though I am the one who once gave them incredible power.

"Even though you all may have gone through the same event, that does not mean that you didn't see it, or feel it, a different way than others." Miss Corbeau states in a calm, soothing voice. "Everyone in this school has faced some form of trauma because of the Crow. Those here are brave enough to talk about their personal experiences with being possessed by the Crow. They have all faced a great deal of pain because of it." My embarrassment is quickly forgotten as she says that last sentence. Pain? I caused them pain? What I did was give them power to get what they wanted; to not be hurt anymore, to be respected, to be feared instead of being afraid. How on earth did I hurt them by doing that? I think through what I'm about to say very quickly, I want answers, but I also don't want to get myself into any kind of trouble either.

"How did he cause you guys pain? I mean,

he gave you superpowers, what more could you ask for?" All the other kids around me suddenly look uncomfortable, as if my question brought back some bad memories for them.

"Just because we got powers, doesn't mean it was for a good reason." Cheyanne states with an almost defiant look in her eyes. At her words, fire seems to erupt into the eyes of all the other kids in the room. "We were given powers to hurt people, and we fell for it. The Crow wanted us to take our anger out on everyone just because we felt bad about things they did to us." I look at them all and I can tell by their faces that they feel the same way as her.

"But doesn't everyone want to be able to do that, to get back at the people who hurt you? It seems to me that the Crow gave you what everyone would dream about having." Jade Elizabeth looks at me with a calm confidence that she never had before I gave her the powers of Tigerclaw.

"Just because you want something, doesn't mean you should get it. You shouldn't hurt people because they hurt you. If everyone thought that you should hurt people who hurt you, then the entire world would be made up of everyone hurting everyone. Sometimes you just need to let things go and realize that it's not as big as you thought, and sometimes you need to change. Sometimes you need to change how you speak, how you act, or how you feel about yourself because you may really be the one hurting yourself." I am stunned into silence by her words, and everyone is watching me as I sit here, confused like a complete idiot. I am so wrapped up by what Jade Elizabeth said that I jump a little when Miss Corbeau speaks up.

"It seems that you are someone who sympathizes with the Crow and what he is doing; is that true Luis?" Even though most adults in this town would be terrified thinking that a kid here in this school would like what the Crow is doing, Miss Corbeau does not seem frightened, or even uncomfortable by that thought. She only looks at me with a calm, reassuring expression that helps me feel a bit more comfortable in this awkward situation. Everyone else in the room though, they have some deep anger in their eyes. I try to only look at Miss Corbeau as I explain myself.

"Yeah I-I guess I do." I hear a few of the other students scoff and groan at my answer and I lower my head, afraid of seeing the hatred on their faces. How did it come to this? Why do my old soldiers hate me so much after everything I did for them?

"Now that is enough everyone." The calming voice of Miss Corbeau instantly silences everyone's sounds of disapproval. "Remember, this is a space for everyone to be able to speak freely without judgement. We must respect his opinions." She looks at me without any negative emotions, as if she has no judgements against me at all. "Now Luis, would you like to explain why you feel that way so that you can help us understand your point of view?" I don't even have to look at the students around me to know that they are holding back a lot of negative words, I can feel the negative vibes just radiating off of them. I clear my throat, trying to make myself feel less awkward, but it doesn't work.

"Well... I guess I just feel like the Crow is giving a person who everyone messes with what they always want, the ability to get back at the people who were hurting them for no reason. Everyone gets picked on at least once in their life, but some people get messed with all the time, and a lot of the time they get picked on for stuff they can't control." Even though I am looking at Miss Corbeau as I speak, I can see a few of the other students around me look away, as if they can see that I'm right and they don't want to admit it. "Everyone wants to get back at those who hurt them, it seems like you guys were given a gift to be able to do that, and nobody picks on you anymore, now do they?"

"They don't mess with us anymore, that's true." I look over at the girl Lexi that I turned into the Flying Ace just last year. "The issue we face is that they don't mess with us because they are afraid of us. They think that we are somehow connected to the Crow and if they do anything to us then the Crow will come for them. They avoid us like we have the plague. Sometimes the only people who hang out with us are people who have also been transformed by the Crow. Only they know what we have gone through." All the students lower their heads, a dark, depressing cloud hanging over all of them. As the silence falls over everyone, I feel my heart sinking into my stomach. I have really hurt these people, haven't I? In so many ways I have changed their lives, and not for the better. Because of their one interaction with me, everything changed for them. I don't know what to do now. What have I been doing as the Crow? Have I done any good in the almost three years I've been doing this? What am I doing with my life?

"Well everyone, I believe our time here is up." Miss Corbeau interrupts my thoughts, nearly making me jump in my seat. I had been so wrapped up in my thoughts that I almost forgot where I was. "Your parents should be here to pick you up, Luis I am very glad that you were able to join us today and I hope you can come again, we meet at the same time, same day, every week. We all would love to hear more from you and see your point of view." Even though she seems to be welcoming to me, all the other students glare at me, obviously showing me that I am not welcomed by them. I told them how I felt, and they didn't like it. They do not like the fact that I support what I am doing as the Crow, even though they followed my orders once. I grab my stuff, trying not to look at anyone as I swing my backpack over my shoulder. I leave the room, staying silent while everyone else chats about what was said during the session, some of them even whispering about what I said, and they do not say nice things about it either.

As everyone wanders past me to go outside to head to their, or their parent's, car to head home, a sudden memory comes to me. I remember who Miss Corbeau reminded me of. It was a while ago, when I was entering some of my artwork into the county fair and I wandered into a fortune teller's tent. She told me things about myself that I would never have told her in a million years, but she somehow knew after talking to me for only a minute. The woman had said her name was Corva, but everyone called her Shadow. She disappeared as if by magic as soon as I turned around to try and talk to her again. I had wondered for a while if she could actually be the human form of the crow Shadow that came from the Crow Medal. I need to talk to her right now.

I run back into the art room, practically ripping the door open in excitement only to see that the lady is gone, leaving Mr. Sizemore alone in there. When he looks up from his papers and sees me, he gives me a teasing grin.

"Hey Luis, did you forget something again?" I look around the room again, but I still see no trace of Miss Corbeau, or whatever her name really is.

"Sorry Sir, I was looking for Miss Corbeau."

"Oh you just missed her, she just walked out the door." Mr. Sizemore gets back to looking at his papers while I am completely confused. I was just outside the door since the end of the therapy meeting, I would have seen her if she walked out the door. Did she somehow get past me even though I was right there, or did she somehow magically disappear? Disappear... just like when I saw her at the fair. Was that her, or am I imagining all this?

I leave the room and slowly walk down the hall, my feet dragging beneath me since I suddenly feel like a zombie. My heart is pounding so hard that I can hear it echoing in my ears. The sound practically fills the entire silent hallway. What just happened? And what on earth am I going to do now?

As I make it outside and get into my uncle's car, I can't find an answer, nor do I think I will ever get one. The car ride home with my uncle is practically silent, I'm too wrapped up in my own thoughts to say anything. I wonder about Miss Corbeau from today and the lady from the fair who called herself Corva, I wonder, but I get no answers as we make it through the winding roads back home.

Chapter Five
Colomba-
Nonna Explains

To combat the cold outside, my dad has built a fire in the fireplace. The three of us are circled around the cozy fire; my dad reading a book while Nonna knits a sweater and I sew together a small hole in a dress. The weather may be cold and damp outside, but in our little house, we are cozy and warm. Nonna smiles at me from over her knitting as she asks me a question.

"So how was tutoring today Tesoro? Do you feel like you got a lot done?" I shrug a little as I finish mending the hole and cut the thread, revealing the fixed dress.

"I guess so, Alex just tried to spend the whole time flirting like usual, so I'm not sure how much of it he retained. Hopefully he learned something." Nonna giggles a little at my remark.

"That boy just never gives up, does he? Being persistent can be good for some things, but not in the game of love. In that game, persistence can be pretty dull." I chuckle at her remark.

"Yeah, that's a good way to put it, I usually just call it annoying, but that works too." Nonna laughs softly, as she examines the sweater she is knitting, measuring it to make sure that it is long enough.

"Don't worry Tesoro, one day he will finally figure out that you are not falling for his tricks and will leave you alone. He can't go on like this forever."

"Sometimes it feels like he can go on forever though, and that would be my worst nightmare. I mean the guy just never shuts up. He's constantly showing off and being a jerk to everyone around me. If I have to live with that the rest of my life, I would probably do terrible things to that guy. He's always talking about how good at sports he is, how everyone thinks he's good looking, and about how much money his family has. That last one is the one that bugs me the most though, he didn't earn that money so why does he get to show off about it? He was just born lucky enough to be born in a rich family, but he puts down people who aren't so lucky and are poor. Why does he think that's okay?" Nonna stops her knitting for a moment to look into the fire with an expression on her face that I know all too well, she is trying to think of a way to say something to me, but is unsure of how to say it.

"I suppose that he, along with so many, was taught that money is the most important thing in life. It is important, do not get me wrong, but it is not the most important thing. Nowadays, children are taught from a young age that money is everything. Money is the only way you can have friends, have a loved one, or have a meaningful life whatsoever. After my long life, I can tell you this with full honesty, that is a lie. Having more money can make life easier, that is true, but it does not make you happy or unhappy. A person needs to find that out for themselves." Nonna shakes her head slightly as if in annoyance. "This boy Alex seems to believe that being rich makes him better than other people. Sadly, many people have that belief. It seems that he thinks that being rich will make you care for him in the way he wants. Obviously, his plan isn't working, many young men believe that money will buy them love, but it does not, having an attitude like that will only attract girls who will take advantage of their money, but never love them. I hope he learns that one day before he gets stuck with someone like that." Nonna looks around the small room, her eyes going over the simple, yet comfortable furnishings and decorations.

"Our family has mostly been poor throughout the years, but we have not been unhappy. We learned to manage through all the struggles by remaining together and trying our best to make things better for each other. That is what truly brings joy. I hope you can always remember that so that you and whoever you end up loving will be as happy as you can." Nonna's serious expression quickly melts as she gives me a grin and a sly wink. "Just promise me that it won't be with this Alex boy, he seems to be a jerk and does not deserve you." My father's attention from his book is finally broken as he chuckles.

"Yeah please don't, I don't want a kid like that in our family. He sounds like he could ruin any family reunion just by opening his mouth." The three of us laugh together as the fire merrily burns in the fireplace, the flames slowly eating away at the logs as they crumble to ashes. The three of us chat, and I keep a smile on my face, but something still gnaws at the back of my mind that keeps me from truly enjoying the moment. My mind thinks about how Alex may truly never give up on me. He has been chasing after me ever since high school started, and we are juniors now, but he still hasn't given up. It's almost scary that he is still chasing me even though I've told him no a million times. Why can't some guys just get it through their head when a girl tells them that they aren't interested? Why do they keep having to chase the girl? The only reason I still tolerate Alex is because I don't want to be mean and I tutor him and get paid well to do it, even if it's like trying to teach a brick wall sometimes.

A sudden thought sends a chill down my spine as I realize a very disturbing fact. It may actually be dangerous for Alex to flirt with me like this since I'm sure that I know of one very dangerous person who also seems to have feelings for me, the Crow. I haven't thought about this in a while, but there have been multiple signs to indicate that the Crow has a crush on me, not me when I am Silver Dove, but the regular me. The Crow has protected me multiple times during his attacks on the school and has shown that he cares about me, even trying to talk to me personally about why he has done certain things, wanting me to feel more sympathetic towards him. He even snuck in through my bedroom window so that he could talk to me when he learned that he is what I fear the most. He even told me straight up that he loves me when he did that. That was one of the most horrifying moments of my life, and he seemed to know that, but tried to make me feel safe with him. Makes me wonder if I am friends with the guy who is really the Crow, or does he just spy on me like a weirdo? With how often Alex flirts with me, I wouldn't be surprised if the Crow already knows that Alex likes me too. With how the Crow acts towards bullies, and since Alex seems to bully practically everyone, I wonder why the Crow hasn't done anything to him personally. I have told hold back a gasp of shock as I realize something obvious, the Crow has done something personally to Alex, he transformed him into the bull like monster last year. Did he do that because Alex bullies everyone, or was he targeted specifically because he likes me and doesn't hide it at all?

I suddenly feel sick as I realize that the Crow probably singled him out because of me. Alex was forced to do horrible things when he was in that form, and it was because he cares about me. I know I shouldn't feel this way, but I feel guilty about all of this. What other things has the Crow done because of me? Who has he hurt because of me?

As the conversation with my father and Nonna starts to die down, I excuse myself and go to my room, wanting to be alone with my dark thoughts. I don't want to disturb their pleasant evening when they notice that I am suddenly not happy anymore. I lie down on my bed and stare out at the back yard, thinking back again to the time the Crow sneaked into my room through that window. I think about how for a month after that I kept the curtains closed because I was afraid of what would be outside. Now I look outside, almost expecting him to be there. I close my eyes, wanting nothing more than to just fall asleep and wake up tomorrow not remembering any of these thoughts I've had tonight, but I know that what is going on in my head will keep me awake for hours. Even though I know this, I lie on my bed, praying for sleep to come.

Chapter Six
Luis-
Shadow's Answers

I slam the door behind me, the sound echoing through the apartment, but I don't care, I need answers. My uncle just dropped me off at the apartment while he went out again to finish some more errands, now is the perfect time to find out what I need to know. Throwing my backpack on my bed, I unzip my jacket to reveal my Crow Medal pinned to my shirt. Placing my hand on top of it, Shadow instantly appears, perched on the windowsill next to my bed. She looks up at me with her dark eyes, her black eyes that reveal nothing to me, hiding her every emotion that she doesn't want me to see.

"Hello Master, how was your day?" I glare at her, knowing that she is just trying to avoid talking about the obvious.

"Let's skip the small talk Shadow, you have a lot of explaining to do." She cocks her head to the side as if she has no idea what I am talking about. Her black eyes still not showing anything.

"And what exactly am I supposed to be

explaining to you? I know that I know many things that you do not that you may want to learn about, but you will have to be specific about what you wish to know." I pause for a moment, trying to figure out if she's trying to imply that I am stupid, but I push that thought out of my mind when I realize that she is just trying to distract me from my mission.

"You know what I mean Shadow, I want you to explain what happened just an hour ago with Miss Corbeau and that therapy session." Shadow lifts her wings slightly in, what I'm guessing, is supposed to be a shrug.

"I believe what happened there was pretty self-explanatory. All the kids you transformed were traumatized by that event, so they needed help. I can understand why, you convinced them to do some very terrible things. The school saw this and hired that therapist to help them, I consider that a smart choice on their part. And it seems that they all have negative opinions of you as the Crow, saying that you are the villain here. I must say that I can see why they would say that." I want to yell at her, screaming that she is wrong, but I stop myself because I know that she is trying to distract me again. I won't let her do that this time.

"No Shadow, explain to me about that woman, Miss Corbeau, who is she?" Shadow stares at me with slight annoyance, as if I am being ridiculous.

"She's a woman that's a therapist that the school hired to help out with this. I don't know what you expect me to say here." I close my eyes and take in a deep breath and release it slowly so that I won't start screaming. When I have had a moment to calm myself, I speak again but slowly, trying to keep myself under control.

"Shadow, she looked just like that lady I met at the fair when I put some of my drawings and such into a competition there, remember? She was the fortune teller who called herself Corva." Shadow just stares at me for a moment, not showing any emotion before she speaks to me in the same slow, annoyed tone that I had used with her.

"So you're mad that these two women... looked similar?" I finally lose it as I sweep my hand across my desk, sending papers flying towards her but she doesn't even flinch, she just continues to stare at me like I am being a stupid little kid.

"You know that's not what I mean!!" I scream at her, letting my rage finally come out. "When I told you about the fortune teller, Corva, I asked if you were her because she said some things that made me think that you could be her! And now here is another lady that looks exactly like Corva who also talks like you! What am I supposed to think about this except that you are her?! Tell me!! Are you those women?! Have you been able to get out of the Crow Medal this whole time and interact with the world while I thought you were stuck in here?!" I point at my chest where the Medal hangs from my shirt, but Shadow doesn't even look at it, she only looks at me, her expression has not changed at all during my outburst. She lets the silence hang between us until I start feeling awkward and look away from her, staring down at my shoes in my embarrassment when I realize how ridiculous I probably look to her.

"Are you done?" I whip my head back up to look at her in shock. She said that to me like I was a child throwing a temper tantrum and she is the parent having to scold them. I am almost hurt by her tone until I realize that she is right to be annoyed, I acted horribly to her, and I should apologize. I lower my head again, feeling ashamed.

"Yes... yes, I am done... I'm sorry Shadow for yelling at you." Shadow nods at me and, I know she can't smile since she is a bird and has a beak, but I get the sudden feeling that she is trying to smile at me.

"I accept your apology, Luis. It has been a while since you have had an outburst like that, you have been so much calmer recently. I feel that you have been maturing a great deal, and I am proud of you for that, but you cannot let outbursts like this happen again, not with me or anyone else. If you want to be loved in this world you must show love, even when you are upset." She sounds like she is trying to be my mother scolding me, but being gentle with it, and she is doing a pretty great job of it because I now feel even more guilty than I felt a moment ago.

"I know, I know." I turn away from her, not wanting her to see how ashamed I feel right now.

"Just because you know it, doesn't mean you will do anything about it. Everyone knows that you shouldn't be mean to others, but still do it anyway. A person needs to learn to be kind and respectful even when upset, that is the sign of a child becoming an adult. You are a junior in high school now, after next year you will be an adult and you will need to act like it. Please remember that or you will be lost in this world." I nod at her, still not brave enough to look back at her.

"Yeah I know, I still have a lot of growing up to do, but sometimes it feels like I am already lost. Everything just feels so unfair. Alex is a horrible person, but he has a family rich enough to buy him an awesome car while my uncle and I are so poor that we can't even replace my winter coat that has holes in it. I get to freeze to death while he gets to relax as he drives to school in his heated car. I can't believe I'm jealous of that jerk." I take deep breaths in and out to try and calm myself, but images of him showing off about his car and money just keeps popping back into my head, only making my anger worse. When it feels like I may have another outburst, I feel something land on my shoulder. Glancing over, I see that Shadow has perched herself on my shoulder. She looks into my eyes with affection and pity, like a person looking at their dog who has gotten themselves stuck in a silly predicament.

"Do not worry about what he has and you do not, because it is quite obvious that you have something that he is jealous of that he could never have. You could have what he has one day, but if he remains as he is, then he will never have what you have." I wait for her to explain, but she remains silent.

"What do you mean? What do I have?" Shadow softly chuckles as if I am missing something completely obvious.

"You have friends, real ones, not the fake ones that he has who only care about his money, his status in the sports teams, or who his family is. You have friends that care about you and encourage you in your life, mainly Colomba, the girl that Alex wants in his life, but can never have. While she willingly stays by your side and talks with you instead of trying to avoid you like she does with Alex." This time I am the one that chuckles. What she said is very true, and I've thought of it several times before myself, but it still feels so good to have someone say it out loud.

"I may have Colomba and the others as my friends now, but it seems that nobody cares about me as the Crow anymore. Just look at how my past soldiers talked about me. I thought I did the right thing, but apparently I was wrong." Shadow gently pushes the hair out of my eyes with her beak, something she always does when she tries to cheer me up.

"It is alright Luis. Our decisions are usually controlled by our past experiences and how those experiences make us view things in life. Sometimes what we get is darkness. We all have darkness that is put within us when bad things happen to us. Some have more darkness than others, some people can cope with their darkness while others cannot. Sometimes the darkness in us wins. Which of those people do you think you are?" It doesn't take me long to figure out an answer to that question.

"I guess, based on what you are saying, I have been letting my darkness control me." Shadow nods slowly.

"It does seem that way." I let out a faint sigh.

"I guess something needs to change." Shadow nods again.

"I guess so too." Outside of my room, I hear the back door opening and my uncle's voice echoes around the apartment.

"Hey Tigre, I picked up a pizza, let's eat!" Without another word, Shadow gives me a silent nod before taking off into the air and flying back into the Crow Medal on my chest. As soon as she is safely in the Medal again, I open my door to go meet my uncle in the kitchen. The two of us have dinner and before I know it it's time for bed.

As I curl up underneath my covers and my eyes start to feel heavy, a sudden though occurs to me, Shadow did not answer my question again. Just like when I asked her about Corva after the fair, she got my mind focused on something else so that I would forget about the question. I want to put my hand on the Crow Medal and summon her again to ask the same question, but my eyelids are too heavy and before I know it, I fall into a deep asleep.

Chapter Seven
Colomba-
Andre

A massive crowd makes its way through the halls of the school as we all head to the front doors at the end of the school day. Everyone is chatting about their plans for the weekend, things that happened earlier today, and just general things, nothing truly special. While the crowd seems to engulf me in their mass, a familiar face comes up to walk beside me.

"Hey Colomba, how's it going?" Luis asks me with his usual kind, gentle smile. I try to smile back at him, but I feel that it is halfhearted. I still keep having those thoughts from last night swirling through my mind about the Crow. I can't get them out of my head no matter how hard I try, and the guilt still keeps the true smile off of my face. Even though I truly feel this way, I lie to my friend.

"I'm doing okay, how are you Luis?" Luis just shrugs at me.

"Okay I guess, not much happened today. Honestly, I'm kinda bored." I chuckle softly.

"Yeah, same. Your uncle is still picking us up today, right?" Luis nods at me and as we walk side by side I think about what I said. It was true, nothing has really happened today, and in our school that is kind of a blessing. It means that nobody got hurt, and the Crow hasn't done anything, always a plus.

When I exit the school doors, I see something that immediately makes me roll my eyes since I have a feeling the peacefulness of my day has come to an end. A small group of people, mostly girls, are hanging around Alex, who is leaning against his new car, obviously showing off his brand new "baby" as I have heard him calling it. The girls around him are simply fawning over him as he tells them all about his car. Why on earth do they care about a car that isn't even theirs? Also, why does having a fancy car make Alex more attractive to them? People don't make sense. Luis and I start walking towards the group so that we can get to the spot his uncle told us to meet him so he can pick us up. From the corner of my eye, I see Alex perk up a bit when he sees me and he lifts his hand up, trying to get my attention.

"Hey Colomba!" The girls he had been talking to also look at me, but they aren't full of welcome like Alex is, jealousy and anger flares in their eyes. The glares they give me send a shiver down my spine. "Hey, c'mon over, I want to talk to you! It's important!" I can see Luis glaring daggers at Alex, I'm guessing he can see that Alex is lying to me so that he can try to flirt again like he always tries to do. Luis is so sweet, he is always looking out for me.

"No thanks Alex, I'm waiting on my ride!" As soon as he hears that, Alex leaves the circle of girls who had been flirting with him to start walking next to me with Luis on my other side, still glaring venomously at Alex.

"If you need a ride home, I would be glad to take you, plus I can take you out for a good time before I drop you off. Sounds like a good deal, am I right?" He looks down at me, his green eyes sparkling with mischief.

"Nope, I'm good. Luis' uncle is coming over to pick us up in a minute." Alex finally glances over at Luis, the mischievous glimmer in his eyes is gone to be replaced by annoyance and anger.

"Ahh, you're letting your uncle pick you up?" he chuckles at Luis as if he finds him pathetic. From the corner of my eye, I can see Luis' jaw muscle clench and his eyes grow narrow as he tries to remain calm despite Alex acting like this. "Are you and your uncle too poor to have your own car Louie? I guess I shouldn't be surprised you guys don't have any money, considering you wear the worst, rattiest clothing I have ever seen." My fists immediately clench, and I am only seconds away from punching him in the face when Luis interrupts me. Luis releases a faint sigh before he instantly lets go of his anger, and looks Alex dead in the eye without any negative emotion whatsoever.

"Well I'm sorry Alex that I don't have a fancy car, but I believe that a man can only be a man if he earns what he has and doesn't get things handed to him. I hope you enjoy your little gift though." There is not even an attempt to hide the sarcasm in his voice, and Luis makes it even more obvious with a little smirk after he speaks. My heart stops for a minute, terrified that Alex will hurt him for implying that Alex isn't a man, but when I look at Alex, I can see that he is just as surprised as I am. Alex looks too surprised to even be upset or say anything. He opens his mouth for a second before closing it again, unsure of what to say considering the guy he always teases actually said something like that to him. He looks away from us to look back at his car, at that moment the anger I had expected is in his eyes, but it isn't directed at Luis. I look over to Alex's car to see that most of the group that had been around it before have gone away, but there is one person that has their hand on the car, looking at it with absolute wonder and joy.

"Hey!! Get your hands off of that you creep!!" The guy at the car quickly removes his hand from it and backs away a few steps as Alex runs back to his car. All the anger I had felt moments before at Alex has been replaced by fear for the guy next to Alex's car. From the look on Alex's face, I'm sure that things are not about to end well. I look over and recognize the guy that had been touching the car, his name is Andre. Andre is well known in school for being a pretty nice guy, but even more well known for being in one of the poorest families in town.

Andre backs away from the car with his hands up, as if trying to say that he meant no harm. This doesn't get rid of any of Alex's anger though. Alex still marches over to him like he wants to start a fight. When Alex reaches his car, he looks down at the spot that Andre had touched, from the way he's looking at that spot with disgust you would think that Andre left a gross smudge all over it, but there is nothing there. When he sees that there has been no damage, Alex looks up at Andre with fire in his eyes while Andre looks as if he is unsure about whether he should stay and talk this over with Alex, or just run away.

"Now tell me grease monkey, what were you doing touching my car?" When he calls him a grease monkey, I remember something else about him. He helps his father fix up cars a lot to help make ends meet. He even fixed my dad's car once or twice now that I think about it. Even from this distance I can see that Andre is shivering slightly at the sight of Alex's rage. I can understand why, everyone has heard about things that have happened to people when Alex has been mad at them. It's easy to see how much damage Alex could cause, with Alex's massive muscles, making Andre look like a stick figure drawing by comparison, it looks like Alex could break Andre in half like a twig.

"I didn't mean anything by it man, I promise." Andre tries to smile at Alex in a friendly way, but Alex only glares back at him. "I just thought that it was a really cool car, I didn't mess it up or anything, you can see that." I can see the corner of Alex's lip twitch slightly as he holds back his anger, and from that I know he is about to do something mean. I start moving towards the two of them, but I know I am too far away to do anything before Alex makes his first move.

"Mess it up? You messed it up as soon as you got near it. You couldn't even dream of affording something like this in your whole life, so you don't deserve to even look at it, let alone touch it. Now why don't you just crawl back into that rat filled hole you call your home and leave the rest of us alone. None of us want to risk getting any of your poorness rubbed off on us." Andre's eyes grow wide and I'm unsure if he is going to start crying or try to fight Alex, but I won't let either of those things happen. I finally reach the two of them and stand in between them, glaring right at Alex.

"What was that, Alex?" Alex looks surprised for a moment, but then smiles at me. I'm confused for a moment about why he's smiling until I realize that he got what he wanted, my attention, and I willingly gave it to him. I mentally beat myself up for falling into that trap when Alex chuckles at me.

"Well Colomba, a man needs to protect what is his, don't you think?" From the corner of my eye, I can see Andre slowly walking away, keeping his eyes on Alex the whole time, trying to be sneaky so he won't be noticed. I'm okay with this, I want him to get away so that he won't get hurt. I won't let Alex enjoy having my attention, I don't care if I'm unkind or not, he deserves to hear the unkind truth.

"That wasn't protecting Alex, that was just rude and mean. And it's not really yours though, is it Alex? Your dad paid for it, it's technically his. Luis was right, a man wouldn't do something like what you just did saying you were "protecting what's yours", a man would earn what he has and still be respectful and not show off what he has. You are just being a stupid child, and you wonder why I never want to ride in that stupid thing with you. I have better things to do than deal with you and all your bragging." I walk away before he can say anything else. Walking back to Luis, I can see him laughing hysterically, he had obviously watched the entire thing. When I get back to him, Luis tries to stifle his laughter, practically having to bite his lip to do so. Even then he is still smiling so big you would think he just won a million dollars. When I look at him trying so hard not to laugh, despite what just happened with Alex, I can't help it, I start laughing too. Seeing that it's safe to laugh, Luis joins me too.

"Jeez, that was harsh Colomba, it was hilarious though. I didn't know you had something like that in you." I chuckle at his remark.

"Well believe it, I can be pretty feisty you know." I hold my hands up playfully like a boxer. Luis grins and holds his hands up in a surrender position.

"No don't hurt me, I give up." I give his arm two quick, light punches, teasing him a little. I chuckle at him as he pretends to act horribly wounded by my strikes. As he moans in his playful agony, I glance over to see that Alex is looking at Luis and I, well not really looking, more like glaring with all the hatred in the universe. Some of the girls that had been hanging around his car before have come back and they are still trying to get his attention, but he isn't even giving them a glance, his eyes are like lasers directed at me and Luis. The scariest part about that glare though is that I don't know who that hatred is directed at, me or Luis. Does he now hate me for embarrassing him like that and basically saying I would never date him? Or is he showing that hatred towards Luis because I am willingly hanging out with him but not with Alex? I have a feeling the hatred isn't directed towards me since I have turned Alex down and embarrassed him a few times, but he always comes back to me, always trying to flirt. No, I'm sure that he is showing that hatred towards Luis. Those two have always hated each other. Luis seems to hate Alex since Alex messes with him a lot, and Alex seems to hate Luis since Luis and I are friends, and Luis is a boy. With Luis being a guy that is close to me, and with how jealous Alex is of any person that's close to me, it's expected that Alex would be angry that I would rather be with Luis than him. Does Alex think we are dating, or at least close to it?

When I look at Luis, I see one of my best friends, could we ever be something like that? Could we ever be a couple? He is the sweetest guy I've ever known, and is always encouraging me to try and do better. Luis always seems to want what's best for me, and tries to always make me smile. He's artistic and funny, one of the greatest people I have in my life. I would be lucky to be with a guy like that, but I can't let myself think like that. He's one of my best friends, I'm not going to ruin that by catching feelings for him when he probably doesn't feel the same way. I can't ruin one of the best things in my life like that.

Luis' uncle's car pulls up and the two of us get

in. His uncle greets us with his confident, charming grin and we head to my home. As I glance out the window, I can see that Alex is still glaring at us like we are his greatest enemies. I turn away from him, scared of that anger. Even though I'm not looking at him though, I can still feel his rage, it feels as if it is slowly burning the skin on my face where his eyes scorch me. We drive away with Luis and his uncle chatting cheerfully, and I try to join in, but my mind is still trapped with the anger that I saw in those dark, menacing eyes.

Chapter Eight
Luis-
Who am I as
The Crow

Colomba hops out of my uncle's car and heads into her house, waving cheerfully at me before she walks through the front door. I wave back at her, trying to be just as cheerful as her, but as soon as she is inside, the smile on my face disappears. After what Alex said earlier, I have had a nagging thought running through my mind ever since, even though I tried to keep that hidden from Colomba. Now that I am alone with Uncle Diego though, it's time to discuss it. I have absolutely no hope that this will actually work, but I can only try.

"Hey, Uncle Diego?" He keeps facing the road, but I can see his eyes glance back at me in the rear-view mirror.

"Yes Tigre?" I look away from his gaze, a little ashamed about what I am going to ask.

"Do you think that I can get a car?" He pauses, so I keep talking, hoping that I can convince him. "I'm old enough to get a license and I will take care of it and everything. That way you wouldn't have to go out of your way to pick me up from school or whatever I can handle things on my own. It would save you so much time, and I can have some freedom to do stuff on my own. What do you think?" I look back up at his eyes in the rearview mirror, but as soon as our eyes meet, he lets his gaze return to the road.

"What brought this up all of a sudden? You've never asked about getting a car before." I fiddle with my hands a little bit, feeling nervous about this entire conversation. I can't tell him the truth, that I want to do this to be able to shove it in Alex's face that I can get a car too, and also that I can be able to go out and do things with Colomba. That would be so awesome to be able to just leave my house, get into my own car, and go pick Colomba up to spend the day together. That sounds like a dream come true to me. I quickly make up something to tell him, wanting to sound as believable as possible.

"Well, you know, I just felt like I'm old enough to be able to take care of things on my own and be able to go out and spend time with my friends without having to work it around your schedule. Besides, I would be able to help out too, and I may be able to get a job too and be able to help with bills and such." As I watch my uncle through the rearview mirror, I can see a familiar look on his face, the look he always gets when he is thinking hard about something, but it is not a pleasant thing to be thinking about. Just from that expression, I know what he is going to say before he even says it.

"I don't know Tigre, a car is a very expensive

thing to purchase, and we don't have that kind of money. Maybe you can earn some extra money so you can get one on your own. I'm sure you can find a cheap car pretty easily, it may need a little work on it, but I'm sure we can figure it out together." He tries to make himself sound hopeful, but I can tell that he feels disappointed that he can't provide me with this. He knows that I don't really ask much from him, so for him to not be able to provide me with one of the only things I have ever asked for must be hard for him. I know that this moment must be hard for him, but I have to keep trying even though I know that this is probably going to fail too.

"What about the money my parents left behind for me? Can I use some of that to get myself a car?" He shakes his head as I hear him release a deep sigh.

"C'mon Tigre, we have discussed this before. That money is not to be touched until you turn eighteen. When you have finished school and become a man, then you can use it. But we talked about it, and we said that you would use that for college first. You can still live with me while you go through school, that should save you some money. Hopefully you can have enough that you can go to school and get a car, but I doubt it would be any kind of flashy car, it would be very ordinary." I hold back the groan of frustration that really wants to come out.

"But I don't want to wait that long."

"I'm sorry Tigre, but that's how it has to be." From his tone, I can tell that this is the end of the conversation. I hold back the urge to keep trying to convince him, because I know nothing will result from it. I turn my head away from him and look out the window, hoping that this awkward car ride won't last much longer. Thankfully, it only takes a few more minutes to reach our destination.

My uncle and I park behind our apartment, and I am ready for today to be over. I already feel completely worn out by this day full of joy and disappointment. It's been almost an hour since what happened with Alex earlier at school, and even though I'm disappointed by the conversation with my uncle, I still have to hold back a grin whenever I think of the look on Alex's face. I have seen Colomba knock Alex down a peg before, but it is always beautiful to see. I just wish it happened more often, I want to see his hurt and disappointment every day. My happy thoughts stop for a moment as I realize how horrible that sounds and I want to take it back, but I know it's true. It's horrible to think, but I like seeing Alex in pain. It's probably natural for someone to like seeing a person they hate in pain, but it doesn't mean that it's the right thing to do. I need to keep reminding myself of this or I might end up just as bad as him, always wanting everyone he doesn't like to be miserable. Sometimes it feels like he wants them to be miserable because he is miserable.

Since I didn't get much sleep last night, and I had two tests earlier today, I am exhausted. Laying down on my bed, I let my eyes close to have a bit of rest before dinner is ready. Almost as soon as my eyes shut, I am asleep, but my mind does not give me peace.

A dull, red light seems to come from everything around me, but it still feels so gloomy, like I'm in a deep cave. Looking around, I can see that I am in Colomba's backyard. In front of me is the apple tree near her garden that is surrounded by flowers. I've painted her here before, for the contest at the county fair, but this beautiful spot now seem distorted, like I am in a twisted, nightmarish version of it. All of the flowers are now a sick red, as if they are made of blood. The grass and tree are rotted and black with death. Rancid apples hang from the tree, looking like disgusting, shriveled sacs of liquid rot. Looking up through the leafless tree branches, I am horrified to see that even the sky has become a sickening red, it looks like this entire world is bleeding.

"Why did you do it?" A soft, gentle, familiar voice asks me, I look away from the sky to see that Colomba is now standing beneath the tree. She is wearing a beautiful white dress, she is the only thing here that doesn't seem corrupted or ugly. She is looking at me with an expression of deep sadness and horror.

"What do you mean?" I ask, my voice barely above a whisper in my fear.

"Everything you have done with your powers as the Crow. You have caused so much pain and fear, even those who followed you and did as you ordered fear you now. How could you do all this? How could you hurt me? I thought you loved me." I try to move closer to her, to comfort her, but she just moves back, getting closer to the dead tree. I stop moving, afraid that she will start running away if I continue to get closer.

"I do love you Colomba, more than anything!"

"Then how could you do this?!" Her sadness is slowly being replaced by anger, it sends a knife through my heart at the sight of it. I look away from her, trying to get the courage to answer her.

"I did it all for you. I wanted to make things better so that I could be with you, so we could be in a world where we would be happy. I love you more than anything, I need you!" Her tiny hands clench into tight fists as her eyes narrow into rage filled slits.

"You have been trying at this for years, but it never worked. Why did you keep doing this if it was obviously not a good plan?! Why would you keep going with this plan of hurting everyone if it wasn't going to get the result you wanted?! Why did you make us all go through that misery?!" My eyes grow warm as I try to hold back the tears.

"I don't know." I say, barely above a whisper. "I guess I just wanted to have the result I dreamed of, so I kept trying, hoping each time that it would work out. I just had to keep hoping or else everything I had worked for would be for nothing." I look up when I hear Colomba scoff at me.

"Oh please, you were just being pathetic!" I feel myself cower a little at her harsh words, not believing that someone as sweet as Colomba could say something so cruel. "You did all that just because you were a petty little boy who wanted revenge on all the people you feel hurt you! You wanted people to suffer! That's it!!" Her voice is starting to sound distorted, getting deeper and growling, almost as if a lion suddenly learned how to speak. "You want me, but you know you can't have me because I want a good man, something you will never be! Why would I ever be with someone as pathetic as you who can't learn to let go and move on with your life! You will always be the loser of this world if you let all those people get to you! And you will never have the love you want either, because no one will want to be with someone so bitter and angry! So why don't you finally give up on me since you know you will never have me!?" The tears start to flow down my face, hearing her say that to me. Does she really think that way? Will she really never love me?

"But I can't give up on you, I can never let you go. I love you and will always love you." I say this in a pathetic little whimper, probably making me look worse in her eyes since she just told me that I was acting pathetically. Colomba just shakes her head at me slowly.

"But I will never love you." With that last bit of pain filled truth, Colomba backs up until she is against the apple tree. As I stand here, completely horrified, I watch as first her hair, then her back slowly being absorbed into the tree until there is nothing left of her. The tree trunk now looks as if it is a little swollen from where it had absorbed her. The swollen portion travels up the trunk and into the branches, like a parasite slithering through a creature's body. When the swollen, slithering bits reach the ends of the branches where the apples are hanging, the withered, rotten apples suddenly start to swell like balloons. I stare up at the swollen apples, confused by what is happening, but that doesn't last long. Reaching up a hand to try and touch one of the apples, it bursts in my face, spraying me with a red liquid. I let out a scream of horror, but no mercy is given to me. All at once all the apples on the tree start bursting as well, covering me and the rancid garden around me in the red liquid. I'm pretty sure I know what the red liquid is, but I don't want to admit that to myself.

When the final apple bursts, and I am releasing one last scream of fear and shock, my eyes fly open, and I jolt upright in my bed. I take in several deep breaths as I look around at my surroundings, wondering where all the red liquid is. It takes me a moment to realize that I am safe, and it was all a nightmare.

I let my body fall back on my bed, my head sinking into my pillow. Closing my eyes, I try to get myself to fall back asleep, but my mind is running through everything that happened, wondering if what Colomba said in it is true or not. It takes another hour or so for me to fall back asleep, but even with all that time passing, I still don't have an answer to that question, and maybe I never will.

Chapter Nine
Colomba-Andre and Angela

The cold is especially bitter today, I only spent a couple minutes outside earlier getting out of the car and then into the school, but my fingers hurt from the cold. It feels like needles are poking my skin, it is that freezing outside. Why is the world so cruel doing this to us? World, why can't you be more kind and make the temperature more bearable, something a little cozy? That would be very nice of you. I wrap my scarf around the lower half of my face, trying to warm up my nose, which feels more like an ice cube stuck to my face. Even though I've been inside a couple minutes, I am still shivering, my teeth are chattering so much that I'm almost afraid that they will break.

I make it to my first class without any issues, but I can see that everyone else is having the same problems as me. Around me people are rubbing their hands together and blowing into their hands to try and get them warmer. When class starts, people still try to do whatever they can to get warmer in between trying to take notes. The aura around the room feels miserable with everyone feeling so uncomfortable. Thankfully, by the end of class I feel a little bit warmer. When the bell rings to signal the end of class, we all rush out the door to get to our next class. The hallway is crowded like always, which is usually annoying, but today it is actually kind of nice. With everyone so tightly packed together, and with all that body heat in one place, it actually warms me up so that I feel normal again. This little bit of comfort brings me joy for only a moment before it is ruined. The smile fades when I see something that I just know will turn into a trainwreck. Coming down the hall, probably coming out of the school's auto shop class based on the car grease on his hands, is Andre, and I can see that he isn't really paying attention to where he is going, and he is about to bump into someone that will make his day miserable, just like she always does, Angela. I am too far away to do anything to prevent it, I can only watch as he bumps into her shoulder, and she turns to face him with the rage of a cornered tiger.

"What do you think you're doing?!" The entire crowd in the hallway stops moving to stare at Angela, everyone eager to see another one of her little hissy fits. It is a popular pastime in our school to be honest.

"How dare you even touch me when you are so filthy?!" Angela basically shrieks at Andre, who stumbles back a bit in surprise at how loud and mean she suddenly got. Andre glances down at his hands to see that he still has quite a bit of grease from the school's auto shop on his hands. He quickly rubs his hands on his old, worn-out jeans, trying to get rid of the grease, while he stares down at his shoes in embarrassment.

"I'm really sorry, I didn't mean anything by it, I just-"

"You just what?!" Angela interrupts, screeching like a banshee while the entire hallway has gone silent to watch the craziness going on in front of us. "You just happened to bump into me with your filthy self while I'm dressed in an outfit worth more than your family's house! Oh please! You just wanted to try and bring me down to your level, but some dirt isn't going to even get me close to how far down you are! I mean, just look at my purse, it costs more than what most people pay for a car." Stepping out of the crowd, I face Angela, looking at her purse with disgust. I can tell that it is a name brand purse, but it does not look good. It has the name of the brand plastered all over it, and is kind of almost in an egg shape, it's strange.

"If you're going to show off so much about how much something costs Angela, then you should at least make sure that what you're buying is worth it. I mean, why would you spend so much money on something so hideous?" Around me I can hear people laughing, but I keep my eyes on Angela because I may have said something dangerous. Angela's eyes are wide in shock at my daring comment, her cheeks are flushed while the knuckles on her hand gripping around her purse are white from having so tight a grip on the bag. For a split second, it looks like she might slap me across the face, and I brace myself to either take it or dodge it, whatever happens, but it doesn't happen. Instead, her tight grip on her purse suddenly loosens as she smirks at me, like she just caught me in something stupid.

"Of course you would say that Colomba, you say that kind of thing because you know you could never buy it in a million years." A few people around me laugh at her words, but I don't let her win.

"You are right, I would never buy it in a million years, because I would rather spend my money on something that looks good instead of that ugly thing." I don't give her a chance to come up with another insult, I just walk away from her while the crowd that had been watching us begins to disperse, heading for their next classes. I can hear some of them talking about what just happened while Angela turns and struts down the hall, her ugly purse swinging at her side with each step.

I want to scream right now, this happens all the time. Someone does something horrible to someone else, and I have to step in to stop them before it gets any worse. I always have to stop them because I know what can happen. The Crow is probably always waiting around for something like this to happen, can't they all see that? The Crow lurks around and waits for someone to do something cruel, that's when he tempts people with the power he can give them. That's how it has happened every time. Why can't they see that what they are doing can cause people to be tempted, to want to get revenge? Why am I the only one who sees sense? Why does everyone refuse to change even though they know that it would be for the greater good?

I wrap my arms around myself, as if trying to comfort myself with a hug. Why do I feel so alone with this task of making things better? Why does everyone seem to only want to make things worse?

I continue down the hall to get to my next class and, even though I have been inside a while now, I suddenly feel as cold as if I were to walk out in the snow. I suddenly feel so alone.

Chapter Ten
Luis-
A New Hope

Just like, what seems to be, everyone in the school, I saw what happened between Andre, Angela, and Colomba. I am hidden within the crowd so none of them have noticed me. Just like always, I am invisible. I watch as Colomba makes her way through the crowd, leaving the situation. She has her arms wrapped around herself, and a dark cloud seems to hang over her. There is a deep sadness in her eyes, as if she has lost all her hope in the world. I want to rush towards her, to embrace her and help her feel better, but as I try to move towards her the crowd seems to be pushing against me, making the distance grow between me and her. I watch her move farther and farther from me until she turns a corner and disappears from my sight. After that, I stop fighting against the current of the crowd and head towards my next class. As I journey there, I make my decision.

    I make it into the classroom right as the bell rings, and I sit in my usual spot. Class begins and we are asked to just do a simple assignment during that time, and I get it done quickly. When I turn in the assignment, I ask the teacher if I can go to the bathroom, and they thankfully say yes. I rush down the silent hallway to get there, it only takes a minute. Locking the door behind me, I open up my jacket to reveal the Crow Medal. Placing my hand on top of it, Shadow appears, perched on top of one of the bathroom stall doors.

"Good morning Master, what made you want to contact me during school hours?" I turn away from her, not wanting to see her reaction when I say what I feel needs to be done. Instead, I look at myself in the mirror. In the dirty mirror, I see a young man with black hair hanging in his face. Behind that screen of hair hide dark eyes that are currently burning with rage. Looking into those eyes, I like what I see.

"I need you because we need to create another soldier, transform me into the Crow." I expect to hear her wings fluttering as she starts flying around me to let me transform, but all is silent in the bathroom. The silence hangs between us for a while until Shadow speaks with a very cautious, stern tone, like a mother questioning a child about something when they suspect that the child did something bad.

"Why Luis? Why do you want to transform someone again? It seemed like you were going to stop doing this and move on to better things? Why are you taking yourself backwards?" She releases a sigh of disappointment before she speaks again, a bit more softly this time, as if talking to herself more than me. "After everything you heard from those you have transformed before in that therapy session, you still want to do it again? I don't believe I will ever understand you, Luis." I turn around to face her, keeping the fire in my eyes as I glare at her.

"You don't need to understand, you just need to follow orders." Even though I am glaring at her with all the anger I feel deep inside and speak firmly, she just looks down at me with pain and pity in her black eyes.

"This is because you saw how sad Colomba looked after what happened with Andre, isn't it?"

"Just do it Shadow!" I feel fury rising in me, but she doesn't stop.

"You always seem to lose your head when you see Colomba in any kind of pain, you always want to rush to her aid, but this is not the way to do it."

"Enough!!" I am breathing heavily now, trying my best to remain calm even though I want to punch a hole through the door of the bathroom stall. "Transform me now Shadow, as your master I command it." Shadow sighs softly, lowering her head in disappointment.

"I thought things were finally changing, I thought you were growing up. I suppose I was wrong, but I will never give up hope for you Luis. You are a good kid, and one day you will realize what you truly need to do. Hopefully this one last failure will teach you that lesson." Without another word, Shadow jumps off the bathroom stall door and flies around me in a fast circle. She keeps flying around me until she is just a black blur swirling around me, faster than any creature could ever be. The wind whips around me, I blink one moment and open my eyes again to see myself as the Crow in the bathroom mirror. I may be the Crow right now, but I don't feel happy like I usually do whenever I transform, now I only feel dread and misery. I turn away from the image of myself and close my eyes so that I can concentrate.

"Shadow, find Andre." Shadow flies out of the bathroom and down the hallway as a shadow on the ground. She flies by several people who don't even notice that she is there. They just go on with their boring, normal lives, not realizing that a magical being has just gone right past them. Shadow goes down hall after hall until she finally enters a classroom where Andre is currently listening to one of the English teachers prattle on and on about some old as dirt book. Shadow flies straight into his angry heart and I let myself be known to him.

Hello Andre. Andre jumps a little in his chair in surprise. Glancing around, he doesn't see anyone near him that could have made the voice he heard.

Don't worry Andre, I am the Crow, and I will give you the revenge you seek. All those who hurt you will feel your pain and more. Those who made fun of you for having nothing will understand what that is like, they will have what they love taken from them. What do you say?

With us possessing his body, I can feel his lips curl up into a cold smile. In his mind, he thinks through multiple memories of people making fun of him for his family being poor, showing off about what they have and telling him that he could never afford it, and telling him that he will always be at the bottom of the world and never be able to improve his life. That last one always hurts him the most, having people think he can't help his family improve their lives. Having people doubt him always hurts his pride. He may not have much in the world, but he will always have his pride, no matter how many people try to take that from him.

Andre must suspect that we can see everything he sees, since he has a clever way to communicate without anyone in his class noticing. He glances down at his notebook, pulls out a pencil, and writes down his wish.

I'm ready, let's go.

My lips curl up into a smile as I let Shadow take him over. A massive gust of wind whips around the classroom, sending books and papers flying. A few people scream as their hair rushes all around them. The entire classroom has fallen into chaos while Andre remains sitting in his desk, smiling calmly as everyone lets out screams of terror, everyone asking what is going on. Andre knows, but he will not share. The teacher tries to calm everyone down, but it is obviously not working, so they open the door to the classroom so that everyone can get out. All of the students leave in a mad rush through the door, like a stampede of stupid animals. They were all so overcome with terror that they did not realize that they left one student behind. This gives him the solace he needs to complete his transformation. Within seconds, he is unrecognizable. My newest soldier has arrived.

Chapter Eleven
Colomba-
The Taker

Class ended a few minutes ago so that we can have lunch. Nat and I stayed behind in the classroom a little longer than everyone else since we needed to ask the teacher a question about a project we are both working on. Thankfully, I think this project will be super easy and we can get it done no problem.

Since everyone else is already either in the lunchroom or in class, Nat and I are alone in the hallway. Our footsteps almost echo in the empty halls. It's kind of creepy. The only sounds besides our footsteps are our soft voices and the sound of the wind howling outside. Apparently, according to my dad, we may have a snowstorm coming in some time tonight. Maybe we can have a snow day tomorrow and not have to go to school. That would be kind of nice to have a little break. Nat and I talk about the stuff we would like to do if we do have a snow day tomorrow; she talks about sleeping in and getting to relax while I talk about a lot of stuff I want to get done, like getting ahead on some school stuff, finishing a quilt my grandmother and I have been working on, and reading a book I've been trying to finish for a while now but never have the time to do with all my classes and extra stuff I do.

As we talk, a blood chilling coldness comes over me and I have the strangest feeling that my calm day is about to get really crazy. As Silver Dove, I've had this feeling many times before and it always means that something bad is close. Whipping my head around, I look behind myself to see nothing unusual down the hallway except for a single figure. Someone dressed in a black cloak, like what you would see in a fantasy movie or something like that. Weird. The figure is walking towards Nat and I, if you could even call it walking since you can't see the person's feet. You can't even see any part of the person's body at all, the hood of the cloak is pulled down low so that you can't see the face and not even their feet poke out from underneath, the cloak just glides across the floor as if there isn't even a physical body there, as if it's a ghost. I lean close to Nat, not wanting to speak too loudly in case the strange figure hears me.

"Hey Nat?" She glances over at me.

"Yeah, what?" I don't even look at her as I respond, not wanting to take my eyes off of *whatever* it is that I'm seeing.

"Do you see that one guy in a black cloak walking over here?" I point down the hallway at the strange figure, and Nat's eyes widen for only a moment when she notices him.

"Yeah I-I see him... should we be scared of

him or something? I'm not really sure how to feel about this? Is this another Crow thing, or is it some idiot who doesn't know how to dress?" I shrug at her.

"Honestly, I have no idea, if he is another one of the Crow's creatures his costume isn't as dramatic as what it usually is. Maybe he's in costume for something. Is there some kind of event going on today?" Nat shrugs at me this time.

"No idea, I thought today was just a normal day." I nod at her as we both continue to stare at the figure as it gets closer and closer.

"Yeah, same, I don't think anything is going on. Maybe he just dresses in a more "interesting" way than us." Nat chuckles at that.

"Yeah, I don't think I would ever dress in anything that "interesting"… Should we run?" I look at the figure for a moment, unsure of what to do, but then it hits me. This person is walking right towards us, they obviously want something from us. If it's a regular person, and we run, we would hurt that person's feelings.

"No Nat, let's just see what they want." Almost as soon as those words leave my lips, the figure stops only five feet from the two of us, just standing there for a second before they whip their cloak open to reveal two gloved hands that lunge towards us, but nothing else. There truly is no body under the cloak, it just floats there as if it is really a ghost. All there is of it are the hands that reach towards me and close around my throat before I'm able to get away.

The fingers are like ice around my neck, it

almost feels as if I will freeze to death if it holds me any longer. I kick and swipe my hands towards it, but since there is no body to attack, my strikes just fly through empty air. When it feels like it will squeeze the last breath from my body, it releases me with a dark, sinister chuckle. I look to my side to see if Nat is still okay, but she is gone, as if she disappeared into thin air. I look all around me, but I don't see a soul, all while the demonic ghost like creature continues to laugh at me. I glare at the empty cloak, filled with more hatred than I have ever felt in my entire life.

"Where is she?! What did you do to her?!" The figure chuckles a moment longer before he answers me in a deep, chilling voice that makes my blood freeze.

"She is gone, I took her, just like I will take everything that everyone cares about. I am the thief that steals what you love, for you that is your friends, we will need to see what everyone else in this school cares about that I will need to take." Oh my gosh, the power the Crow gave him, it's to take what you love the most?! What kind of sick mind must the Crow have to give this guy a power like that?!

"Who are you?!" My simple question causes the specter to just laugh at me again in amusement.

"I am the Taker!" The specter shouts before he laughs maniacally again before disappearing with a wave of his dark cloak. The hallway is silent now, as if nothing unusual has ever happened here. Even though my mind is racing, my body is as still as a statue, so confused and so broken by what just happened, by what I have lost.

Chapter Twelve
Luis-
Missing and Broken Hearted

Everything is still calm and quiet in the school, but I smile with the knowledge that it will soon break out into chaos. My soldier is wandering around the school now, searching for his first victim. I am not looking through his eyes at the moment, and am currently just myself instead of the Crow. I want to walk around and see the craziness for myself. I also have Shadow with me as well, she is currently hiding in my jacket. She stated that she wanted to be here too, but not for the same reasons as me, she said that she wants to be here to help counsel me when this plan goes wrong.

I almost want to chuckle at that thought, she thinks that I will fail again. Shadow may not have any faith in me, but I believe that I can succeed. All these people will pay for how they hurt Andre for something he can't control, but more importantly, they will pay for how they have hurt Colomba. She is such an empathetic person. When she sees someone in pain, she feels their pain, she tries to help people, but can't because no one else cares. She has to suffer with these people, but I won't let that happen again. Colomba is so gentle and kind, she doesn't deserve to be in any kind of pain. She deserves to be in a better world. I will create that better world for her. I smile thinking about her, but that joy does not last.

As I wander through the empty hallways, all of a sudden, it feels as if I have been dunked in a pool of icy water. A violent shiver comes over me and I look over myself, but I don't see anything wrong with me. That was the strangest feeling I have ever had in my life. It almost felt like I was dead for a moment, like I was almost gone. Opening up my jacket slightly, I look down at Shadow who is nestled in a pocket on the inside of the jacket.

"Shadow, what on earth was that?" She looks up at me, a sad look in her black eyes.

"Your little project found his first victim, it just so happened to be Colomba." My heart plummets in my chest, but Shadow doesn't show any mercy and continues to explain, her voice cold and irritated. "You gave him the ability to take whatever you care about the most. Colomba is a sweet girl who doesn't seem to care about material possessions, she cares the most about the people she loves. You are one of them, you would have disappeared too if you weren't the one in possession of the Crow Medal." I feel my eyes widen and my heart race as a single, beautiful thought runs through my mind. I'm one of the people Colomba cares about the most. That happy thought is shattered though when I realize the obvious, I just made the girl I love lose all of the people she cares about. Her friends, her father, her beloved grandmother; they are all gone because of the person I created. I am probably the worst person on the face of the earth right now. My legs feel wobbly, and I put my hand out to hold onto a locker beside me to keep myself standing. My gosh, I truly am a monster, just like Colomba always says that the Crow is. I think back on the therapy meeting I had walked in on and everything they all said about me, it is all true. Keeping myself steady by holding onto the locker, I slowly let myself crumple to the ground as tears fall down my face, my body shaking with uncontrollable sobbing.

After all the effort I have put in my mission to try to help people as the Crow, I have done nothing good. All the people I have transformed even admitted that to my face when I went to that meeting. I have failed, I'm a loser and a failure just like how everyone has always told me that I am. What have I done, what have I done to the girl I love, one of the only people in the world who has ever accepted me? It feels like I have done more bad things to her than anyone in this school, yet I still act like I am friends with her. It almost feels like I am tricking her by doing this, remaining her friend while constantly hurting her with my soldiers. People in this school and all over town say that I am a bad guy who creates monsters, but they are wrong. I am a monster creating monsters.

While I am sitting on the ground, sobbing like a little child, Shadow squirms her way out of my jacket and perches herself on my knees so that she can look me right in the face. Her black eyes stare into mine as if she is waiting for something.

"What?! What do you want?! Do you want me to tell you that you were right?! That I was wrong?! Is that it?!" She stares at me a little longer in silence, as if she is trying to make me uncomfortable, which is working.

"No, I don't have to say anything, you already know the answers to those questions. You know that what you did was wrong. You took away the most precious things in the world for the girl you love. Everything you have done as the Crow has been wrong, all three years you have had the Crow Medal has gone to waste. Sometimes I am surprised that the Medal chose you. Sometimes I wonder if you truly have a good heart worthy of it." I stare at her, completely stunned into silence. Shadow has scolded me many times in the past, but she has never said anything so cruel before. When I look into the blackness of her eyes, I can see that she is being honest with me, just like how she always is. I should have listened to her a long time ago.

Without anything else needing to be said, I feel myself crumble on the inside. My head collapses into my hands as I start to bawl my eyes out as if I have just lost everything in my life, to be honest I kind of have in a way. I cry hard, not even caring if anyone walks down the empty hallway and makes fun of me for being a crybaby. I couldn't care less if they do. I am too broken to care. I stay like that, crying on the floor like the loser I am as Shadow just watches me from her perch on my knee. I don't know if she is staring at me with pity or disgust, I am too afraid to look up at her to see her expression. The two of us stay like that for what feels like eternity as I cry like a man who has lost his whole world.

Chapter Thirteen
Colomba-
All Gone

Running through the halls, I can see some people crying as if they just lost the most precious thing in the world to them, and I know that's the truth since some people are screaming about how they lost their most precious thing in the world. It's not that hard to figure out. This guy the Crow has created, the Taker, moves pretty fast, I haven't been able to catch up to him at all. It's obvious that I'm going to need to transform into Silver Dove as soon as possible to be able to see more of this guy and hopefully defeat him. Some more people are coming out of the classrooms, trying to figure out what all the racket is from all the people in the hallway. As I look closer at the people who are upset because they have lost something important, I see some faces that are familiar to me.

Sitting on the ground against the wall, crying their eyes out, Angela wails like she has more pain than anyone who has ever existed. I can see that all the expensive things she usually wears to show off are now gone. The fancy, ugly purse she was showing off to Andre earlier today is gone as well as her usual nice jewelry, fancy clothes, and pricey accessories. All she has now is a dingy, grubby looking sack that she is wearing like a dress. It almost looks like one of those old-fashioned potato sacks made of burlap. I am almost tempted to laugh, she always shows off about those fancy things, and now that is gone and it's almost as if she has nothing left in her life if she can't have these things. As if the only thing that is important about her is her stuff.

There is a person sitting near Angela that looks familiar to me, but I can't quite tell who it is. They are familiar, yet something is also different about them which is making it harder to recognize them. The guy is very scrawny, so weak that it looks like he can't even pick up a book. They are shabby, dirty, and not very attractive looking. They almost look like they have never really taken care of themselves their entire life. In other words, they look like a pathetic mess. This person isn't crying like Angela, they are just sulking on the ground, looking like a little kid who just got put in time out. This person glances up for a moment to see me looking at them, and they try to hide their face from me.

"Don't look at me Colomba, I don't want you to see me like this. I look terrible. Please just wait until Silver Dove fixes this, then we can talk." I almost jump back a little in surprise when I recognize the voice and finally figure out who he is, it's Alex. Apparently, he thinks that his attractive, strong body is what he values most. I can understand why he doesn't want me to look at him right now because if that's what he values the most in life then that is just really pathetic.

I let my eyes scan the hallway as people continue to cry and moan about what they have lost. Glancing back again at Angela, a sudden thought hits me. She was just making fun of Andre earlier today about how he has nothing, and now the Crow has created a creature that can take away what you care about and has now taken away what Angela loves the most. Andre must be the Taker, it's the only person I can think of where that would make sense.

A sudden thought hits me, and a new wave of terror comes over me. Pulling out my phone, I call Nonna, praying that what I think is wrong. Please, please let me be wrong. As the phone tries to get ahold of Nonna, I impatiently wait to hear her voice, I need to hear her voice and know that she is okay. When her voicemail starts to play, I know the truth and I feel like I am about to either faint or throw up. I know what has happened to her now. When the Taker touched me, he didn't just take my friends away, he took my family too, he took everyone that I love. She is gone, the woman who has been a mother to me my whole life has disappeared all because two selfish young men, the Crow and Andre, decided they wanted to make people suffer. Well, they've had their sick fun, now it's my turn to make them suffer for what they have done, for the pain they have caused so many people. An uncontrollable rage comes over me that I have never felt before. More than anything, I want to make Andre, the Taker, feel the pain that I am feeling now.

Turning away from the weeping crowd, I walk

away from them, down the hallway. I need to find a place where I can be alone. Silver Dove needs to appear and make things right again. Nobody even notices me as I leave them, I walk alone to make sure they won't be suffering for much longer and the ones I love can be returned to me. There are only two people that need to suffer now, the Crow and the Taker.

Chapter Fourteen
Luis-
Decisions

My tears are starting to slow down, and my heaving sobs have become just quiet little sniffles. I am incredibly grateful that we are still alone in this part of the hallway, and nobody saw me like this. They already make fun of me enough, I don't need to give them one more reason to tease me. Throughout my little crying fit, Shadow has remained perched on my knees, silently waiting for me to calm down. When she sees that I am starting to stop crying, she finally speaks.

"Are you ready to fix your mess, or are you going to remain here feeling sorry for yourself about something you caused?" Her tone is cold, but I can understand why, she's right. I did cause this mess, just like all the other messes I have caused with my powers as the Crow, they were all because of me. I take in one last pathetic sniffle before I speak to her.

"What should I do?"

"Exactly what I said, fix your mistake like an adult and make things right. Take away the powers you have given to this young man, transform into the Crow and make an announcement to everyone that you are sorry for what you have done and resolve to change. After that you need to get in contact with Silver Dove, you need to work together to improve the world, that is your destiny, that is why the Crow Medal chose you, that's why they were created in the first place. Do what needs to be done." I nod my head, terrified of the thought of doing all the things she said I need to do, but knowing that she is right. I need to just follow her orders like my soldiers have always followed mine. Speaking of which, I should probably talk to my soldier now. Closing my eyes, I let my mind connect to my current soldier. Through my mind, I can see that he has reached out his hand to grab another unsuspecting victim, a rather pretty girl, and as I watch, the girl's skin suddenly gets covered in pimples, her white teeth turn a disgusting yellow, and her nice hair suddenly becomes greasy and lank, falling around her face looking like damp seaweed. Apparently, she valued her looks above everything else. When the Taker lets her go and she sees her face in the reflection in a window, she screams and runs down the hallway as the Taker laughs deeply, sounding like the specter he looks like. I open my mind so that I can speak to him.

Taker!

My soldier immediately stops laughing and I feel his body stiffen, almost like he really is a soldier trying to stand at attention in front of their commanding officer.

"Yes sir, what can I do for you Crow?" I usually feel very happy when my soldiers talk to me with such respect, since nobody my age usually ever shows me any kind of respect, except Colomba and her friends. Even though I usually feel that way, now I just feel sick hearing it.

It's time to stop all of this, I will be removing your power now.

Within an instant I feel his mind panicking at the thought of losing this ability I have given him and not getting his revenge. He is terrified of what will happen to him when people realize he is the one who did all of this. He's afraid that they will try to get revenge on him, and possibly hurt him for what he's done, for what he's taken from them. I sigh softly, knowing that I would be terrified too in his situation. I need to reassure him that everything will be alright and that all the things he took from everyone will be returned as soon as he loses his powers.

Don't worry Andre, I will-

I don't get to finish that sentence because as soon as that last word is said in his mind, I feel a powerful force hit him from the side and he is thrown through a wall and he falls to the ground, looking like a beaten up rag covered in rubble from the broken wall. The Taker moans a little as he lifts his head, shaking off some rubble from his hood so that he can look up to see who had attacked him. As soon as he sees who it is, his body begins to shake in terror. Flying above him, their wings flapping gently as they glare down at the Taker, is Silver Dove. The two look at each other for an entire minute in silence, the Taker looking at her with fear, and Silver Dove glaring at him with pure rage. Silver Dove is the one to break the silence.

"You took away what I care about the most, and you did that for so many others as well. You are going to pay for that." Wait, the Taker stole something from Silver Dove? I haven't been paying attention to what he has been doing, so I only know of one person he has used his powers on, and that was Colomba. I know that it would be impossible for Colomba to be Silver Dove though. Colomba is much too kind and gentle to be Silver Dove, and she would never go against me, would she? She doesn't really like the Crow, but approves of Silver Dove. Could she be-? No, of course not. She could never be Silver Dove.

Silver Dove lunges forward, trying to grab the cloak that is the Taker's entire body now. The Taker screams in terror before trying to swipe his ghostly hands at her, trying to grab her again, to take away something else she cares about. Oh no, what can I do now?

"Quick! Take his powers now!" I hear Shadow scream as I watch through the Taker's eyes.

"I can't change him back now, Silver Dove could accidentally kill him with her super strength. We just need to ride this out." I say this, but as I watch through the Taker's eyes, I wonder if he will survive until then. Silver Dove keeps lashing out at him like she is facing the person she hates the most in life. I can only sit back and watch as I wait for an opening so that I can change him back. As I do this, I can't help but wonder what he took from her to make her so enraged. In all our battles, I have never seen such fire in her eyes, this is a new kind of fury.

Chapter Fifteen
Colomba-
Fighting the Taker

My fists fly at the ghost like figure in front of me, but my fists just hit the fabric this creature is made of. The Taker laughs at me in a deep, maniacal tone that reminds me of old-fashioned movie villains. Even though I know that my strikes aren't doing anything, I still punch at this strange creature. I want it to feel pain, I want it to be in as much pain as it has made me. He took the people I love, my family and my friends. He doesn't know what it feels like to have everyone you love taken from you all at once. I need to make sure that he doesn't make anyone else feel this way. I need to stop him, and I need to do it now.

As I strike him, tears fall beneath my mask and my breathing becomes uneasy. I take in gasps of air as my silent tears turn into pitiful sobbing. My fists stop flying as my wings grow still and I crumple to the ground in a tearful mess. The Taker reminds floating above me, looking down at me. Even though he doesn't have a face, I feel like he is staying still and watching me because he is very confused by what he is seeing, and I don't blame him. If I saw the hero of the school crying like a baby in front of me, I wouldn't know what to do either.

"You t-took everything f-from me." I manage to mutter through my uncontrollable sobbing. "How- how could you do such a horrible thing; how could you take them from me, my friends, my family? You took everything that mattered to me." For the longest time, silence hangs between the two of us, the silence is so uncomfortable that it makes my skin scrawl, it almost feels like something is moving all over my body. I want to scratch all over to try and get rid of that feeling. When the silence feels like it is becoming unbearable, he finally answers my question.

"I had to, I needed to show them that what they were doing is wrong." He almost sounds like he is trying to convince himself with his explanation, like he needs to remind himself why he is doing all of this. It must have worked because his soft tone is quickly replaced by a voice filled with anger. "I needed to show them that they couldn't mess with me just because I have less than them! They would mess with me just because my family is broke! I work hard to help my family get any money we can! It's not my fault that my mom got cancer and we spent all our money to help her get better! We sacrificed everything for her, and we don't regret it, even if we have to scrape everything we can to take care of the bills every month! I would do it all again if I had to!" Some of the pain in my heart leaves me as I realize just how much Andre has sacrificed, with everyone picking on him because his family doesn't have money, it probably feels like everyone is bashing him for everything he did to save his mother. I almost feel bad for him... almost. I look back up at him, letting no more tears cloud my eyes.

"Just because you are in pain and have lost things, doesn't mean you should steal from others to have them feel the same way. You should be ashamed of yourself. You are where you are now because you were afraid to lose your family, but because you made a deal with the devil, I have lost my family, you stole them from me." I stand up again and look underneath his hood as he slowly backs away from me. He probably fears the hatred that I am directing him through my eyes. I unsheathe my sword and point it at the phantom, ready and willing to use it on the monster who stole my family from me. "Now I will show you what happens when you steal what someone loves the most."

The sword flashes forward and the creature swiftly swoops out of the way and then flies down the hallway, looking like a massive bird flying away from something that terrified it. I smile at that thought, yes he is fleeing from something that terrified him, me.

Opening my snowy white wings, I take off like a rocket, chasing after him as if my life depends on it. In a way, I guess it does, without my family and friends, I don't really have a life to live. With my speed, it doesn't take me long to soar through the halls to find him. He rushes past the art classroom, and I push myself to go faster. As I get closer and closer, my heart pounds like a drum in my chest, my hate urging me to go even faster. When I am only inches away from him, I smile coldly as I swing my sword forward, slicing through the edge of the Taker's cloak.

A haunting, anguished shriek fills the hall as the creature scurries away from me, moaning and crying out like a wounded animal as I stay put, letting my wings fall still so that I can land. As soon as my feet touch the ground, I bend down to pick up a scrap of black fabric that had been part of the Taker's costume. I stare down at the scratchy piece of worn-out fabric, not believing what I am seeing.

What have I done? If he had been human in that moment, I would have killed him. How could I have done this? I have never done anything like this before, I'm not usually the one who strikes out at people, I'm the one who is always defending people, not hurting them. What have I done? What have *I* done?! I am a monster! I just tried to hurt someone because I was in pain, I lashed out at one of the people I swore to protect in this school. I have broken my promise and I have done something just like what the Crow and all the people he transformed have done, I have acted out in rage.

My fist tightens around the bit of cloth that used to be part of the Taker as I feel myself beginning to cry again. I am not crying from my rage and loss of my family this time though. Now I cry because of my misery and the loss of myself. I have lost who I am in this fight, and I need to remember who I really am or else I can not get through this battle and come back as the same person. I need to remember what I have always been fighting for, to keep everyone safe, even the ones that the Crow has transformed, they need more help than anybody.

I keep the tears from flowing though, I know that I have a mission to complete, and I won't let my emotions get in the way of that. Putting the piece of cloth within my armor, I open up my wings and take off after him, the desire to see my friends and family again, and the desire to stop everyone's pain is now what is driving me forward instead of my anger.

My wings glide around corners of the narrow hallways as I search, but it doesn't take me long to find him. The Taker is just floating in front of a window, as if he is waiting for me. I soar towards him, but instead of trying to attack me, he just puts his hands out in front of him in a stopping gesture like he wants me to wait. What is this?

"Silver Dove wait!!!" Even though this is probably a trap, I stop flying and land gently on the ground around twenty feet away from him just in case he tries to do anything. I lower my sword so that I can let him speak. I'm curious to see what he will have to say. "I want to tell you that I am sorry for what I have done. The Crow and I both realize that we did something horrible and want to stop it." I blink several times in surprise, not believing what I am hearing. The Crow is sending an apology to me through one of his creatures? The Taker doesn't give me any time to contemplate this since he continues to speak to me. "I should have never taken your family from you, and I shouldn't have taken everything from everyone else either. I was wrong. Please give me a chance so that I can return to my normal life and try to have forgiveness for what I have done."

I stare at him, unsure of what to think as I look at this mysterious figure. I don't know what to believe.

Chapter Sixteen
Luis-
Apologies

Silver Dove stares at the Taker in complete surprise, as if she can't believe that one of my soldiers is apologizing to her, and is telling her that I am apologizing as well. Honestly, I can't believe it either. After everything we have done to each other, it is pretty unbelievable.

After a minute of silence between the three of us, Silver Dove's expression suddenly softens, and I know that she believes what we have told her. She puts her sword away with a gentle smile as she walks closer to the Taker, slowly and cautiously. She walks until the two of them are standing right in front of each other and she is looking at him right under his hood. Since I am seeing through the Taker's eyes, it almost feels like she is looking into my eyes, and I am very uncomfortable with that. It almost feels like she is looking straight into my soul, and I don't think I want her to see the kind of person I really am on the inside. I have a feeling that she would be disappointed if she saw what I truly am, and for some reason, I don't want her to be disappointed in me. Why do I feel that way?

She stares deeply under the hood with that same gentle smile. In a split second, a thought occurs to me that could change everything. She is so incredibly close to my soldier, and I can still communicate with the Taker right now. This is the closest she has ever been to one of my soldiers without being defensive, she has let her guard down. I can have him rip off her helmet so that I can finally see who she really is. I practically scream into the Taker's mind in my excitement.

Taker! Rip off her mask now while she is vulnerable! Do it now!!!

I feel the Taker's mind going through what I have said, they consider doing it for only a split second before that thought leaves their mind and I feel a sense of peace come over him, like a wave washing away mud to create a clean surface again.

"No Crow, I will not." Silver Dove's calm demeanor instantly becomes confused, not knowing what he's talking about since she did not hear what I said in his mind. The Taker backs away from her a little and closes his eyes and I feel the familiar sensation of being ripped away from something. I break my connection with him since I know what is about to happen; he's about to turn back into Andre, he is giving up his powers. I turn back into my usual self as I angrily pace back and forth across the bathroom.

This was another disappointing failure, but something is different this time, something about what happened won't leave my mind. Silver Dove had been so close to me and had looked right into my eyes through the Taker. That was the closest look I've had to her face. Even though I can only see a little of her face through the holes in her mask, I could see her eyes more clearly than I have ever seen them before. They are a bright, clear blue, almost like the ocean. She has calm, gentle eyes. Eyes that make you want to believe everything she says because those eyes say that she will never hurt you, she wants what's best for you. Those are the kinds of eyes I wish I could have. Looking at myself in the bathroom mirror, I only see angry eyes, eyes that show misery. As I look into those eyes, they become even more hostile as I get frustrated with myself. I know those eyes! I have seen them before; why can't I remember who owns those eyes?! This is probably the most important question I have ever asked in my life, but I can't think of an answer no matter how hard I try! Why am I so pathetic that I can't do something as simple as this? Why can't I figure out who she really is? The two of us have been fighting each other for almost three years now and I don't think either of us have realized who the other is, or are even close to figuring it out.

She has an excuse for not being able to figure it out, I barely show my face around her and instead she has to face my soldiers while I am hidden, but I have no excuses. I get to see Silver Dove every time she appears in our school since I get to see through the eyes of my soldiers. And when she is doing "good deeds", as the news likes to put it, all over town I can still see images of what she looks like on the television, so I should be able to figure it out. I mean she has to go to our school or else she wouldn't be able to stop my soldiers so quickly, and I doubt she's a teacher or anything, she seems too young for that. With a school this small you practically know everyone, or at least recognize their face, so why don't I recognize her?

I've heard so many people spread rumors about who they think Silver Dove really is. I've heard these people list practically every single girl in this school, except for the obvious ones, like nobody has guessed Angela since you would have to be nuts to think that a girl like her would ever do something selfless or try to save anyone except herself. Even though I've heard so many guesses, I don't have one of my own that actually makes sense to me. Nothing makes sense to me at all.

Taking in a deep breath, I try to calm myself before I head back out into the hallway. I need to make it look like I am relieved that this is all over, that I am happy that the Taker failed. I need to be happy when I really just want to cry in frustration. After all my experience with hiding these emotions, I almost find it easy to do this. Practice makes perfect I suppose.

Pushing open the bathroom door, I can see that people have already noticed that my soldier has surrendered. They are running down the halls, cheering like they have seen the greatest thing to ever happen in the history of humanity. I plaster a smile on my face as I pretend to be happy and join them in the cheering even though I wish all these people would still be cowering in terror. I want them to finally listen to what I've been trying to tell them for so many years, I want all of this to change. I want to finally feel like I am winning in this life, instead of constantly being the loser everyone has always told me that I am.

Chapter Seventeen
Colomba-
It's All
Over

As I stand there, the Taker opens his arms out like he is expecting a big hug right before he is engulfed in the bright light that I am now so familiar with, the light indicating that someone the Crow has transformed is returning to their normal self. Using one of my wings to shield myself from the light, it only takes a moment for the light to die down and I remove my wing to reveal Andre as his usual self. He looks like he is feeling a bit awkward, I think I can understand why; it must feel weird standing in front of the person you stole practically everything they care about and then gave it back. It must feel a bit scary for him as well since he has given away all his power while I stand before him, still holding on to an extreme level of power compared to him, and I had been attacking him mercilessly in rage only a few minutes ago. He's probably wondering if I will do anything to him, I mean he did steal my friends and family from me, I suppose most people would want to cause him some kind of pain after he did something like that. I am not most people though.

Walking up to him, I notice him flinch a little in fear, but I pretend not to notice. I walk in front of him until we are face to mask, and I rest one hand on his shoulder, smiling in a comforting way to help him relax. I can feel how stiff he is from his fear beneath my hand, but when he sees that smile, he begins to loosen up.

"Thank you Andre, you did a wonderful thing just now. It takes a lot of will to give away power like that." He smiles at me, still looking a bit awkward though. Yeah, it would feel pretty weird getting complimented by the person who was beating you up a little bit ago. "Can you explain something to me though," the worry instantly returns to his face, "what did you mean when you told the Crow that you wouldn't do something right before you turned back into your regular self?" Andre turns his face away from me, as if he is embarrassed by what happened.

"He was telling me that since you were so close to me, and had put your weapon away, you were vulnerable, so he wanted me to…" he pauses for a moment as if unsure if should finish his sentence. He appears to gain the courage since he takes a deep breath to reveal it to me. "He wanted me to take off your helmet." I feel my heart stop in my chest as those words sink into me.

I was so close to having my true self be discovered. If Andre had just felt slightly different about the situation, the Crow would have found out who I am. What would he have done if he found out that I'm Silver Dove? Would he come after me and my family? Another thought comes into my mind when I remember something. The Crow seems to have a crush on me when I am my normal self, he has at least shown signs that he does. He has saved me from being trapped while the Sprinter was causing chaos, he prevented the Giant from doing anything to me when he had me in his clutches, and during Halloween when he created his last monster when he saw that I was terrified of him when his creature transformed into him, he came to visit me to try and explain himself so that I wouldn't be afraid anymore. He even told me that he loves me, I don't know if that was a lie or not, but it could be true. Maybe it would be a good thing if the Crow figures out who I really am, maybe he would decide to stop doing all this since he may actually listen when he realizes who I really am. Should I do that? I don't know what to do.

Glancing back up, I can see that Andre is looking at me with confusion, and I realize that I have probably been stuck in thought for a minute or so, leaving him in a strange silence. Clearing my throat, I smile at him, trying to look reassuring since my silence probably freaked him out a little.

"Thank you Andre for not doing that, the school will be grateful for what you have done. If the Crow realized who I really am, me and probably everyone I love would be at risk. I cannot explain in words how much what you did means to me. I hope that you won't regret your decision." Andre smiles back at me.

"Don't worry, I'll be alright. Having the power

the Crow gave me felt nice, but after seeing how much pain you were in, I couldn't handle it. I have lived my entire life not having the things I want so my family could survive, and seeing you lose your family, it was too much." I lower my eyes from his, a dark feeling coming over me. Whenever I have faced a person as Silver Dove, I usually help the person get rid of whatever issue that caused them to want to side with the Crow. When Jade Elizabeth became the Sprinter because she was shy, I helped her in martial arts to help her feel more confident. When Kal became the Giant because he was overweight, I helped convince him to become healthy. And when Rosie became the Black Iris because she has autism, I helped her by making her realize that she wasn't what everyone said she was based on what they think autism is. With Andre though, I can't do that, I can't just make Andre's family's poverty go away. That is something his family will need to solve, I cannot fix this problem and that makes me feel useless as a hero for him. All I could do was stop him, but I can't give him the assistance he truly needs. I want to look away from him because I feel guilty, it feels like a knife is being stabbed into my heart. I can't help this person who truly needs help. I try to smile at him, and I place my hand on top of his shoulder, trying to be reassuring.

"Good luck my friend, even though it may not look like it, I will be watching over you, so you will be safe." With those parting words, I turn away from him, open up my wings, and take off down the hallway. I need to transform back into my normal self before everyone starts to realize that the danger is gone and start flooding the hallways. Turning down a few corners, I find a janitor's closet and thankfully find it empty. Closing the door, I transform back into my regular self. As I look over myself in a little mirror hanging on a shelf of cleaning supplies, I don't see the usual expression of joy and victory I usually feel whenever I have defeated one of the Crow's followers. Today when I look at myself, all I see is misery. Not only was I unable to truly help Andre with his problem, but I had been willing to really hurt him. I had slashed my sword at him and cut a piece of his cloak off. I had been willing to kill in that moment, and I am ashamed of what I could have done. I could have been a murderer today.

I know that he took my family and friends from me, but that is not an excuse for what I have done. There is no excuse. There will never be an excuse. I am just lucky that I didn't hurt him when he was his normal self. When I look in that mirror, I see a disgrace, I see a person unworthy of wearing the Silver Dove Pin that I was given. I'm surprised that it even worked for me after what I did, since it only works for those with a good heart. After what I did, I don't think I could say that I have a good heart anymore. Slipping out of the janitor's closet, I make sure that I am not seen before I leave it and start walking down the hallway.

As I look down the hall, bright balls of light instantly appear and disappear within a matter of seconds and in their place are things that I'm guessing the Taker had stolen from people. When certain people see these items reappear, they rush over to them and hold them tight, so glad to see it again. In front of some lockers an expensive looking, but ugly, purse appears and Angela rushes over to it, hugging it in joy as relieved tears start to fall from her eyes. She starts talking to the purse like a long-lost friend while I back away slowly in confusion and fear. Wait… wait a minute, everything is reappearing. I look around, waiting for my lost joy to come back. Right beside me, another ball of light ignites, and I have to close my eyes due to how bright it is, when I open them again, Nat is standing beside me looking absolutely terrified. The second she sees me, her terror vanishes, and she wraps her arms around me in a tight hug.

"Oh my gosh Colomba!! You're not going to believe where I was!! I was stuck in this room that was all white and didn't have anything in it except a table! On the table was a cake, I tried to eat some but it wouldn't let me! The cake was a lie! The cake was a lie!!!" I can't help but laugh a little at her as tears start to stream down my face, so overwhelmed with happiness to have my friend back.

"It's okay Nat, I'm here, everything's okay." The two of us hold each other tightly, almost afraid to let each other go. We stay in that embrace for what feels like ages, but was probably only a few minutes, until a familiar voice shouts out to us.

"Hey guys!" Nat and I reluctantly separate so that we can see Luis running down the hallway to us. When I see him, my heart races in joy knowing that I have him back after the Taker stole him from me. I rush over to him, he wraps his arms around my waist while I wrap mine around his neck. Luis lifts me off my feet and swings me around in a circle, the two of us laughing in relief and bliss. More tears fall down my face, I feel so overjoyed to have my friends back. I can't stop crying as Luis and Nat tell me all about what happened after the Taker made them disappear, and I'm glad that they can talk now since I am too speechless from my tears to be able to say anything at all. I can only listen as I am so wrapped up in my joy with having them back that I couldn't even think of anything to say if I wanted to. All I can do is listen as I try to pull myself together after this emotional rollercoaster of a day.

Chapter Eighteen
Luis-
Decisions to
Be Made

The sun is beginning to set, but that can barely be seen due to the storm clouds covering the sky. Apparently, the snowstorm they said could come through is actually happening. The chill that has been hanging in the air for over a week now is now bitingly cold. Stepping outside for five minutes makes your skin feel like it is getting stabbed by a million needles, it is that cold. Even though I have been inside for a while, my hands still feel a bit numb from having to walk around a bit to do some errands for my uncle before returning home. Even though my hands feel off, it didn't stop me from drawing the Taker into the sketch book with all of the other people that I have transformed over the years.

In the sketch I have depicted the Taker floating over the school, he is shown to be far bigger than the school, and having his hands over the school like he is about to do something terrible to it. As I finish the last bit of shading on his cloak, I can't help but feel the same misery and disappointment I felt earlier today when I had realized what I had done to Colomba, as well as when the Taker didn't take off Silver Dove's mask when I told him to. He was so close to revealing her identity to me. Why couldn't he just keep listening to me for just another few seconds longer?

I guess that I will be able to find out her secret identity sooner rather than later though since I will probably be joining her side any day now. After everything that has happened, and what Shadow has said, it might be best for me to just stop doing all this stuff as the Crow and do all the stuff Silver Dove has been doing, you know saving people and all that. Might be what is best for me anyhow since I have never succeeded once with my plan and have only made myself miserable with my failures. I guess it is time for me to move on and start a new path in my life.

When I have finished the sketch of the Taker, I put it in my hiding spot in my desk and then place my hand on top of the Crow Medal. Shadow instantly appears perched on top of the pencil cup on my desk. Her dark feathers almost seem to glow in the faint light of the desk lamp beside her, making her kind of look almost unearthly. Well, I guess more unearthly than she usually does as a magical talking crow. I smile gently at her, not sure how she will speak to me after what has happened today.

"Hello Shadow." Her face remains emotionless as I greet her, and it doesn't change when she responds to me.

"Good evening Luis." Her tone is cold, and I can tell that she is still disappointed with me that I tried to have the Taker unmask Silver Dove. "What did you wish to speak to me about? Is anything else wrong?" I usually look away from her when I feel like I need to say something uncomfortable for me, but this time I look straight into her eyes. She needs to see that I am being honest with her.

"Well I wanted to say that… that I believe that…" despite knowing what needs to be said, I can't find the words to say it right. My words keep getting stuck in my mouth, but I need to tell her how I really feel. Taking in a deep breath, I decide that I just need to say it outright or else I may never be able to say it at all. "Shadow, you were right. You were always right. I should have listened to you from the very beginning. I never should have done all this as the Crow, transforming people like I have. I was wrong." As I stare into the dark abyss that is her eyes, I am surprised by what I see. I expected her to have a smug look on her face like how most people would in this situation when someone admits they were wrong and the other person was right, but instead she looks as if she is proud of me. She flies off her little perch and lands on my shoulder. Without a word, she takes her wings and embraces my face, trying to give me a big hug with her tiny bird body.

"I have been waiting so long to hear you say that, Luis." Her voice almost sounds like she is holding back tears of joy, and I have to admit that so am I. "You have come so far in your journey with the Crow Medal; you have faced pain and misery as well as joy. I have watched you begin this journey as a young boy and start becoming a responsible young man. I have been so proud to watch this change come over you. You have made mistakes along the way, as to be expected in life, but you learned from those mistakes and have come out alive no matter what has happened. I am so happy that you have finally learned from this mistake." I smile at her, gently wrapping my arms around her little body to try and give her a hug as best as I can despite the size difference.

"Thank you, thank you so much Shadow for sticking with me as I was going through this and never giving up on me. I know most people would have by this point." I release her from my soft embrace so that I can look at her face, as I look into her eyes, I try to find answers.

"But what am I supposed to do now? It's not like I can just contact Silver Dove and say that I've changed, after everything that has happened between us, she would never believe that. She would just think I'm trying to trick her or something. Silver Dove would never believe that I could ever change." I look away from Shadow, saddened by what I'm about to say. "I have hurt Silver Dove way too many times for her to ever think of me as anything other than an enemy."

Shadow rests her wing on my hand in a comforting way, like when you rest your hand on someone else's to try and make them feel better.

"Do not worry Luis, Silver Dove has a good heart, I can sense that. When she sees that you are being honest with your feelings, she will welcome you onto her side. She would be so happy that you have seen sense and want to fight the evils of the world with her. I would recommend waiting a little bit before you contact her though." I raise my eyebrow in confusion.

"Why?" She glances away from me as her feathers fluff out a little in discomfort, after all my experience with her, that lets me know that she feels a bit awkward about what needs to be said.

"Well you did make her friends and family disappear today, she may still have some negative feelings that could cloud her judgement. So perhaps just wait for a week or so for her negative emotions to die and she will welcome you with open arms." I smile awkwardly at her.

"I guess I see what you mean. I'll wait for her, hopefully you're right and she will be okay with me after all of this." I pause for a moment as a sudden thought occurs to me. "Hey Shadow?"

"Yes Luis." I feel my body tense at the uncomfortable thought running through my mind.

"When Silver Dove and I join forces, we will probably show each other who we really are, won't we?" Shadow looks as if she is confused as to why I am so disturbed by this question.

"Yes, it would make sense for you two to show each other your true identities. Why do you ask?" I take a deep breath, trying to help myself not throw up as I say this truth.

"Well you told me that those who wear the pins, Silver Dove and I, are supposed to be together, like fall in love. So that means when we join sides and show each other who we really are, I'll be seeing the girl that I will end up falling in love with, right?" Shadow suddenly seems to realize why I probably look like I'm about to get sick. She hops up to my shoulder and rests her face against mine, trying to comfort me like a faithful friend.

"Do not worry Luis, it is always nerve wracking knowing that you will meet the person you will end up with. You want to make a good impression, you want them to realize how you truly feel about them, and that can be difficult for a human being to do. It is difficult for us to do such things since that means opening your heart to someone and hoping they don't harm you. We want to protect ourselves, but we also want to open ourselves to someone we care about, that is very difficult to do but I believe you can accomplish it." I move my head slightly so that she can't rest her face against mine, and she has to look directly at my face as I slowly shake my head at her.

"That's not what I'm concerned about Shadow, not at all." I look over at my desk where I have the initial sketch of Colomba that I drew when I was making the portrait for the county fair. I look at her face in the sketch, right into her perfect eyes, and I feel my heart break at the sight.

"What about Colomba? I can't be in love with any other person besides her. She is the only one for me, I've known that for years now. How could you expect me to love another girl when you have seen all that I have gone through with Colomba? Tell me that." I look at her intensely, but she doesn't look away, she gives the same intensity back to me with her black eyes. My spine chills at the sight of those dark eyes.

"I merely tell you that this is the way it has always been, you will always be with Silver Dove as the Crow, no question. That has happened countless times over the centuries, you will not be the exception. It will be a happy union, just as it always has been, you will find joy with this Silver Dove, I know it." I shake my head at her again.

"I can't Shadow, I know that I can't. I could only be truly happy with Colomba." Shadow releases a soft sigh through her beak, probably annoyed at the realization that I'm not going to change my mind about this, that I will never give up on Colomba.

"So you say Luis, but I have been around a long time, staying with those with the Crow Medal, and things do not change. I hope that you will be okay with how things will turn out." Shadow flies into the air and goes straight into the Crow Medal, leaving me alone again with my thoughts.

Looking around the room, I feel more alone than I have felt in a long time, the walls seem more like the cages of a cell. I am trapped within the destiny that has been given to me by the Crow Medal. I stare out the window as the first snowflakes begin to fall from the black sky. At first there are only a few snowflakes, and then a flurry of them, until finally they come down in an endless stream that turns the dark sky into a waterfall of white. I sit and watch as I wonder about what will happen and if there truly is a way to stop it. As I think about what Shadow said though, I have doubts that I can break this cycle with the Crow and Silver

Dove. If centuries worth of people couldn't break the pattern, I doubt that I can. I watch as the snow falls heavily onto the street below and I try to let my mind go blank and get away from these frightening thoughts as I let myself disappear into the white nothingness.

Chapter Nineteen
Colomba-
The Storm
Moves In

The sunlight tries to break through the thick clouds, but it is unsuccessful. The snow still manages to fall even though it has been going nonstop since last night and is still going strong this afternoon. Naturally, with all the snow we did have a snow day today and didn't have to go to school. Thank goodness for that, it gave me some time to finish up some projects that I've had unfinished for a while. I've been keeping track of my friends to make sure that they are doing well through all of this. Nat didn't answer my messages until around noon since she slept in, she says that she's doing alright and feels fantastic after that long sleep. Luis says that he and his uncle are doing well too. He says that he has been working on some art projects since we have all been stuck inside. He sent some pictures of it to me, and I was super impressed. He had sketched a picture of a mountain with a snow leopard leaping from some rocks with a rising sun in the background. Since he did it all in pencil, it didn't have any color to it, except the dark blue eyes that he added to the snow leopard. He said that he saw all of this in a dream he had last night, and when he woke up this morning, he knew he had to draw it. To say it was great would be an understatement. It looked so realistic that it was almost a photo. I told him so and, just like usual with Luis, he didn't believe me and said that it was just "alright". I swear this boy has no idea just how amazing of a talent he has, I hope he realizes it one day so that he can really do something with it in his life. Until then, I will keep encouraging him and letting him know how awesome he is. I told him that he really needs to put that picture in the art contests at the county fair this summer like he did last year, he will definitely win again. With talent like his, there's no way he can lose.

For me, I spent the day catching up on homework, finishing projects that will be due soon, finishing a book for my English class, and worked on a quilt with Nonna. The one we are working on is super complex and beautiful, it has crazy patterns full of flowers and bright colors. We plan on putting it in a few quilting contests soon to earn some extra cash. Even if we don't win, we can sell it for a good price, people are always willing to pay good money for nice handmade things.

Right now, it is late afternoon, and I am sitting in my room, watching the snow falling as I think about everything that happened the other day with the Taker. I really lost control with him. I don't think I have ever lost myself like that before.

Looking back, I am scared of what I did, but I am absolutely terrified of what I could have done. When I realized that he had not only taken my friends, but also my family, it felt like I lost control over the calm, collected person I have always been, and I released a monster inside of myself. Have I always been hiding that part of myself, or was it created in that moment? The second I realized what really happened, I was willing to kill him for what he had done. Is that normal? Is that something the world could have forgiven me for? Would they have understood why I did it if I told them, or would they say that I am the monster for killing him even though he did something terrible to me? My body suddenly feels as cold as the icy day outside when a chilling realization hits me; I sound just like the Crow.

Whenever I have talked with the Crow he states that he is the victim, that he only does all these terrible things because he needs to show people "justice", when in reality he is just getting revenge on people who have hurt him. He says that he is the one always getting picked on, and so he has to get revenge on those who have hurt him, and he gives powers to these other kids so that they can do the same thing. He makes himself sound like the victim, when he is actually the one who has done something terrible, just like I was doing. Am I really becoming like the Crow? Am I turning myself into a monster like him?

I close my eyes, taking away the view of the snowy backyard so that I can truly focus. I cannot change what I have already done, that is obvious for everyone, but I can make sure that I learn from this moment. I need to make sure that this never happens again. Whenever anything like what happened with the Taker happens again, I need to remember this moment. I need to remember what could be lost if I give in to the dark feelings I had earlier today. If I give in, I lose who I am, and I don't know if I can ever really get myself back from that. I will be lost forever. After what I have already done though, I wonder if Andre could ever forgive me for what I did when he was the Taker.

    Thinking about Andre, I realize that I should probably check up on him to see how he is doing. Pulling out my phone, I get onto A-Streamer and look up his name so that I can look at his page. When I am done typing his name, I see a link to his profile, but also a link to something else with his name on it. I catch my breath in fear as I click on it, terrified of what it may be. Did someone post something awful about him and put it here to try and hurt him after what happened yesterday? When the page opens up to me and I start reading what is there, my fear slowly melts into joy as I read each word. Apparently, a lot of people heard about what happened with Andre as the Taker (obviously, news this big travels fast in small towns like Drew's Hollow) and they found out that he was getting made fun of for being poor, and most of his family money problems come from his mother's medical debt, so some kind people decided to help. Someone has created a page to donate money to help the family pay for the debt. The page has only been active for less than a day and already has over a thousand dollars raised. Smiling, I donate five dollars to the fund. My family may not have much money either, but I feel like we should always help those who are less fortunate, even if you can only give a little like me. I hope that this money can really help Andre and his family, they deserve it. They have all worked so hard to help his mother with her illness and then afterwards to try and pay for the medical debt. Now that they have this extra money, they hopefully won't have to work so hard anymore. They deserve some time to relax in their lives and be able to afford things to help make their lives easier. I'm glad that even though I couldn't really help Andre as Silver Dove, the community stepped up and helped him instead.

    It's wonderful that with Andre they actually helped him, sometimes it feels like I am the only one helping these people out that the Crow has transformed. I've noticed this quite a bit, but a lot of the people that the Crow has transformed are usually avoided by other people. Sometimes I have seen people move to the opposite side of the hallways when they see one of the Crow's previous soldiers. I try to talk with them as much as I can to help them feel less alone, but sometimes I fear that isn't enough. Thankfully, I have noticed that the people the Crow has transformed have sort of banded together to form their own friend group. It is really nice to see them do that, it's nice to see that they are helping those who have been transformed like themselves, letting them not be alone. Sometimes that's the greatest gift you can give somebody, not letting them be alone. I just wish that the rest of the world could see it that way too. I wish that everyone else in the school would stop acting like these people have some sort of terrible disease or something. After all the stuff they have gone through, they deserve better, they deserve to be accepted by the world, not brought down by it. Everyone deserves to feel safe and accepted by others. Even if they have made a mistake and may have caused some pain, if they try their best to make up for it and truly feel sorry then they should be given a second chance. Forgiveness should be given in so many cases, in some cases no, but most should be given forgiveness. I can only wonder how their lives have changed since they were transformed by the Crow, it has probably not been changed for the better though. I have a feeling that they may be a lot more lonely than before. I just hope that pain won't stick with them as they grow up and leave high school.

My entire soul seems to darken as a thought runs through my mind that I haven't thought of in a long time. What happens when the Crow and I are no longer in high school. I mean, this is our third year of high school. Senior year is next year, and then we graduate. What then? Will he keep transforming people at this school so that I'll have to stay in town to constantly have to stop him? Or will he leave Drew's Hollow and cause mayhem somewhere else, and I'll have to follow him wherever he goes to protect whoever he goes after next? Will I have to give up my dreams of going to college and becoming a doctor so that I can protect the world from this maniac? Will I have to give up everything just because this idiot doesn't know how to use his powers like a responsible person? How long will I need to suffer because of him?

There must be some way to convince him to stop this, to join my side and we can work together to make the world a better place. How can I do that? A sudden thought hits me, and it feels like I have been given the greatest idea the world has ever seen, an idea that could change everything in my school. Silver Dove may not be able to convince the Crow of anything, but Colomba might. A few months ago, when he transformed that guy on Halloween, afterwards the Crow came into my room and revealed that he loves me. He says that he did all of this as the Crow for me, to make me love him back, to have me think of him as a good person. He wants me to feel safe around him and want to be his girlfriend. If I could somehow find a way to contact him as my usual self, I might be able to convince him to stop all this. If he loves me as much as he said, then if I ask him, he might stop after some convincing. It will take a lot of persuasion, but we can get there. Then he will show me who he really is, and I can help him move past all of this.

Problem with this plan is that when he reveals himself and we start working through these issues he has, he will probably expect me to start dating him based on what I said when he showed up at my house on Halloween. When he came to my room, he said that he has loved me since he met me and that he did everything he did as the Crow for me, but he believes that I could never love him as the person he really is. I wanted to see if I could convince him to reveal his identity to me, so I told him that I might be able to love him if I knew who he truly is as a person and showed me how he really feels. He believed what I said at the time and almost revealed his face, before my dad interrupted us and he ran off. With this plan in mind, I sort of regret saying that now. After everything he has done, I don't think I could ever love a man like him. I know that I was thinking about forgiveness and how it should be given only moments ago, but like I thought earlier, some things should not be forgiven. With all the suffering and fear he has caused; I could never forgive him. He stole my family from me earlier today, that cannot be forgiven.

What if I do talk to him, I convince him to become a good guy, and then he starts trying to make a move on me and I have to tell him that I'm not interested in him; would that be enough to send him over the edge and make him want to be the bad guy again? I wouldn't put it past this guy to be that petty to be honest. If things don't go his way, he might just become evil again and I won't be able to get it right again since he will probably blame me for him going bad again since I said I didn't love him. So does that mean I would have to pretend to love this guy? And if I do that, how long do I have to pretend? Will I have to pretend to love him for the rest of my life? Would I have to marry this guy to keep the act alive and make sure he doesn't destroy the world because I don't love him? My blood seems to freeze like the snow outside at the thought of being trapped with that psycho for the rest of my life. With all the crazy stuff he has done,

I doubt he would be a good husband or be fun to hang out with. I would constantly be worried that he would get angry for the smallest of things and do something stupid. He seems like the kind who would do that.

So should I try to talk to him as Colomba? It might be worth a shot. I mean I know that I will be safe since he seems to care a lot about me, and I doubt he would hurt me. That means that I just need to wait until he reappears as the Crow to try and start something, then I will make my move. I just need to be patient and wait to see what he does next. I will probably have some issues trying to find him since he always seems hidden, but I guess if I just approach one of his creatures as myself and start speaking to him, telling him I want to speak with him, he might appear. He seems to be able to see through the eyes of the people he gives powers to, at least that's what some of the people he has transformed have said, so he will hear me calling to him. I just need to keep myself alive long enough for him to arrive while being around one of his creatures. That could be a bit difficult if I am going to remain in my usual form and not have the invulnerability of Silver Dove. I can only hope that the Crow will quickly tell his follower to not hurt me, to wait to do anything else until he got there.

There is another possibility though for what he might do. Instead of coming to me himself when I approach his creature, he might ask the creature to "keep me safe" somewhere, in other words, keep me trapped somewhere until the creature is done rampaging. I mean, he has done stuff like that before. When the Sprinter accidentally hurt me, he came himself and carried me to a safe spot and then trapped me in that room so I wouldn't get hurt while the Sprinter continued to run around and cause chaos. And when the Giant was catching people to put in his cage, the Crow told him to put me in the cage as well, but to make sure that I would not be harmed or else something bad would happen to the Giant. So would the Crow bother to try and talk to me, or would he just "keep me safe" until he is done with his "fun"?

    I think this through until Nonna yells out that it is time for dinner, I leave my place at the window to go to her and my father to have a pleasant meal together. We all tell each other about what we have done today and our plans for tomorrow, but I don't tell either of them about the plans that I have for the Crow. My father does not know anything about me being Silver Dove or how the Crow feels about me, but Nonna does. She knows everything about me as Silver Dove, but I don't think I can tell her this part, I know that she would just be too worried about me and will try to convince me not to do it. I have to try this though, it might be my only way to stop all of this.

    The meal ends, and night has fallen, leaving the snowy backyard dark, but the white snow seems to glow in what little light is shown by the moon that is just starting to peak out of the clouds. After doing so much stuff today, I go to bed a little earlier than usual. I still have a lot to do tomorrow, so I'll need all the rest I can get. Even though I want to sleep, my mind won't let me. My brain is still going through the plan I thought of earlier, going through every different little detail that could happen. It all feels like way too much, but I know I can do it. It will be difficult, but I've gone through worse before.

As sleep finally comes over me, a familiar scene passes through my dreams. I am flying through the sky as a dove. As soon as I notice this fact, I know what is going to happen. I have had this dream multiple times since I became Silver Dove. I, as the little dove, flies down into a garden courtyard with the fountain with three people on it; a girl and two boys each with some kind of bird with them. Beneath a willow tree in the garden, I notice a crow and I fly through the branches to get to him. The two of us exchange a little bird embrace and the crow is overjoyed. The joy doesn't last though when the shadow in the sky, once again, destroys the happy moment. The crow gets in front of me to guard me from the creature even though the crow is afraid of it too. The shadow flies towards us, crashing through branches of the willow and as it comes towards us with its massive claw-like shriveled hands it swats the crow out from in front of me and pins the crow to the ground. I feel myself shiver, knowing what is about to happen. The creature grabs ahold of me in its strange claw like hand, but it holds me gently. The three of us hold still as the massive shadow leans in closer to me, and speaks to me in a deep, calming voice.

"I will be coming for you soon, my love. I am almost out of here, just wait for me." When the words leave this strange creature, he leans in close to me, as if he wishes to kiss me. Beneath the claws of this creature, the crow starts to struggle against his grip again, cawing out to me in panic. The crow is terrified for me, as if the crow thinks a kiss from this strange creature would be a fate worse than death. I don't feel that way though, I feel so calm and so happy that we are about to share this kiss. When the creature's lips are almost touching mine, the shadow is suddenly hit by the light through the willow branches, and he is suddenly engulfed in a beautiful golden glow. The light is so bright that it blinds me for a moment. I fly out of the creature's grip and land on the ground so I can be away from the glow, I use my little wing to shield me from the light. My eyes squint to try and see what is happening to the shadow, but now I only see a figure in the light. Within the blinding light is a figure of a humongous creature with large wings that seems to cover my entire vision. With the light and the wings, the only thing I can think of is that this creature must be an angel. It is shaped almost like a person with wings so that would make sense. I do not get to find out though because the creature before me lets out a piercing shriek, not in pain, but in triumph. I stare in awe at the creature, hoping and praying that I can finally see its true form, so I can finally see what has been invading my dreams for years now. I look at the creature within the bright light as it comes closer to me, but when it feels like I am about to see what it actually is, the dream ends. I open my eyes, and I am back in my room.

    My breathing is heavy as I look around, realizing that it is all over now, and the strange creature is no longer with me. My body slowly relaxes as I bury my face in my pillow, trying to forget about that dream even though I know that I will always remember it. I've remembered each of the dreams involving this strange creature. Each time it's the same thing with only a few things added at the end. I feel like this dream is supposed to mean something, but I can never figure it out. I know it's stupid to think that a dream means something since, you know, it's just a dream, but I can't help thinking that there's more to it that I don't get. Maybe I keep having these dreams because the magic of the Dove Pin is trying to tell me something. What am I missing? Does this mean that the Crow is going to be doing something big some time soon? Maybe one of his creations is more powerful than him and causes trouble for him and I have to solve it. Or maybe it could be worse. Maybe something new is coming, something I will be powerless against? That would be terrifying, especially since there have been multiple times where some of the people the Crow has transformed were almost too much for me. To have something new that's even more powerful than the Crow would be next to impossible for me to solve.

When I think back on the emotions I felt during that dream though, I am even more confused. The crow in the dream was terrified of the creature, but I felt safe with it. It was as if I knew that the creature would not hurt me, I knew that the creature cared about me and would rather die himself than let me be hurt. As I go through how the creature acted, and what he said to me, it almost feels as if he loves me, and when I think about how I felt, I think I felt the same way about him in that dream. What on earth does this dream mean? What is going to happen?

Don't miss the previous books in The Adventures of Silver Dove series. Check them out at elizascalia.com.

Eliza Scalia is a therapist who has a master's degree in Clinical Mental Health from Troy University. She enjoys reading, writing, and needlework. Eliza has been writing since she was in middle school and has self- published the Death's Assistant series for young adults.

www.ingramcontent.com/pod-product-compliance
Lightning Source LLC
LaVergne TN
LVHW012113070526
838202LV00056B/5710